The Vessel

ROBERT M WHITBEY

Small Town Hero Series Book #2

DEDICATION

This book is dedicated to my sons, Dylan and Jack. May years from now I hope you're remembered for the amount of good you've done in the world.

Preface

If you haven't read the first book in the Small Town Hero series, The Angel, fear not. Each book of the series is its own story. However, there will be characters and events that you will find in common. Call them Easter Eggs if you like. In fact, Inferno, the short story found at the end of this book, is based on events in the first book. So, don't read that unless you have read the first book.

What you will notice in this book is a lot of direct connections to the Holy Bible. Please keep in mind as you read this that it is a work of fiction. My intent is not to use this as an interpretation of Holy Scripture. It is fantasy, pure and simple. Now, if reading this causes you to open a Bible, well, I don't consider that a bad thing. Enjoy!

-Rob

P.S. While it is not necessary to read The Angel first, you should definitely read it afterward.

Prologue

Sheila ran as fast as she could down the dark alley. She had lost both of her stiletto heels two blocks ago. She screamed for help again and again but no one was around LoDo this time of night, except people who didn't want to be seen. She had run past several homeless men passed out on trash heaps, but they were in no shape to help even if they wanted to. She was alone in her fear.

The thing that chased her flew above her, then behind her, then above her again. It was playing with her! Tormenting her! She hadn't gotten a good look at it as it seemingly jumped from shadow to shadow. It made a high pitched squeal every now and then, causing her to run a little faster each time. But she was tiring fast. She hadn't had a fix since the afternoon, and it was after two in the morning. She felt sick from running so hard, and sweat poured off of her.

She rounded a corner and saw two men getting in a car. She ran towards them, offering them whatever they wanted to take her with them. They just laughed and told her to tell it to her pimp. She reached the passenger side window just as one man closed the door. She pounded on it, pleading. He angrily reached for his knife, but when he turned back to the window she was gone.

"Crazy broad," he said to his friend. "You know what it is? Too many Californians in Denver now. Place is gettin' weird." As his friend nodded in reply, Sheila's body landed on their windshield, shattering it. She was missing both arms and had a large hole in her chest where her heart used to be. Now it was the men's turn to scream.

Chapter 1 – The Streets of Laramie

The alarm clock went off three times before Dylan Mathis decided to get out of bed. He had been setting his alarm to go off thirty minutes earlier than he needed since he was a teenager, just so he could wake up slowly. He wasn't sure why he did this, but it was now a habit. Rolling over, he sat up and put his feet on the cold tile floor. His eyes still weren't open.

Dylan stood and walked to the hallway bathroom, dragging his hand along the wall as he did. He reached the sink, turned the water on and splashed cold water on his face. Finally, he opened his eyes and looked at himself in the mirror and smiled. Another habit he had since he was a kid, and he didn't know why. Maybe his mom had taught him, but he really didn't know.

He got himself ready for work the same way he always did: a quick shower, a shave, then he brushed his teeth. He walked into the small living room and turned on his iPod. Eighties punk rock blared through the attached speakers as it did every morning. He returned to his bedroom and dressed. Light brown pants, blue long sleeved button up shirt, dark tie, and comfortable brown sneakers. He wore the same combination every day to make getting ready for work easier.

Next, Dylan went into his kitchen and poured himself a mug of coffee. He added creamer and a few marshmallows. That trick he learned from his mom for sure. He took a sip and grabbed a blueberry bagel from an unopened bag. He split it and spread some cream cheese on it from the refrigerator and added some jelly to the top and put the two sides together again.

He walked back to the living room, taking a bite out of his bagel. Here was the only surprise he ever had in his morning ritual. It was late April in Laramie, WY, and that meant you could have any type of weather imaginable. Rain, snow, sunshine, fog, or even ice was possible, and sometimes all in the same day. He opened the blinds, revealing what appeared to be the beginning of a beautiful day. Of course, looks were often deceiving in this part of the world. It could be bright and sunny, and still be thirty degrees outside. He looked at his weather station on the window sill and was happy to see it was already fifty-five degrees at eight o'clock. *It might actually be warm by the afternoon*, he thought.

He grabbed his jacket and messenger bag, and headed to the bus stop. His rented home was near the college where he worked, but just outside his normal walking distance. The campus shuttle stopped nearby and he usually caught it for the five minute trip. It pulled up just like clockwork and he got on, nodding to the driver whose name he forgot.

A few students were already on the bus, their faces buried in their cell phones. Dylan took his normal seat near the rear and stared out the window. He owned a four-wheel-drive truck, but rarely drove anywhere. The exceptional public transportation was one of the reasons why he had taken the job at Bridger Community College. That, and there were not many openings for Astronomy professors these days. The pay wasn't high, but it didn't cost much to live in Laramie.

The shuttle stopped right outside the building containing his small office and lab. Though the building was only twenty years old, the architecture looked much older. It had been built to match the historic feel of the area with its prominent use of brick and tall, lush trees. Inside, it was definitely the 20th century. Many wealthy sons and daughters of Wyoming had donated millions to the technological upkeep of the facilities at BCC. They had all the latest technology and he would even have personal access to a state of the art telescope being built high in the surrounding Rockies forty miles outside of town. Of course he had to share it with the University, but that was fine with him.

Entering the building, Dylan stopped to talk with Neville, the overnight janitor who was just finishing up and readying his backpack to go home. The College went out of its way to hire veterans whenever possible, and Neville was a former Marine. He had suffered a traumatic brain injury that had slowed his mental faculties a bit, and the large horseshoe-shaped scar on the top of his shaved head was off-putting to many at first.

"Anything to report, Corporal?" Dylan asked in his best authoritarian voice.

Neville pulled off his ever-present headphones and snapped to attention, responding, "perimeter is tight, all floors are secure, sir!" There was a slight slur to his voice from the injury, but hardly noticeable after you spoke with him for a while.

Dylan returned the salute and Neville relaxed. It was the same question and response every morning.

"It's about time for the bus to pick you up, isn't it?"

"Yeah, but Steve the driver called me and told me he was running late." Neville looked around then quietly said in all seriousness, "he's Air Force."

Dylan chuckled but Neville didn't. They spoke for a few more minutes but were interrupted by the loud horn of the bus. Neville did a quick salute, then quickly walked to the door and was gone.

Dylan took the stairs to his 2nd floor office. He preferred the stairs because of the perpetually cold temperatures in the building. He walked by several open doors, saying a quick, "good morning" each time as he made his way down the hall to his office and lab. As he opened his door, all of the motion-activated lights came on automatically, a cost-cutting feature in all the rooms of the building. He sat his things down and opened the side door to his lab. He looked at his watch and thirty seconds later the technology inside sprang to life.

"Right on time," he smiled.

While the lights in his office turn on when they detect movement, the technology in his lab was set to automatically come to life at precisely eight o'clock. The computers began to hum as the data from the previous night's sky watch was downloaded and analyzed.

Astronomy had changed so much in the last thirty years. Using the internet and remote sensing equipment, one could obtain data from telescopes around the world if you knew the right people. Dylan had a lot of friends as the Astronomy community is tightly knit. Thus, he routinely received data from a dozen telescopes on multiple continents and hemispheres, including the current local 'big one' owned by the University of Wyoming twenty-five miles southwest of town.

He went back to his desk and started looking through his emails. Lots of junk, no personal correspondence. He scrolled and deleted and scrolled and deleted some more. He stared at the screen for a moment as his vision began to blur.

Suddenly there was a loud knock on his open door that made him jump a little. He turned to see his girlfriend, Patty, standing in the doorway. Patricia Nielsohn was a graduate student working on her PhD in Early American History. They had met when she took an astronomy class he was teaching as an adjunct at Campbell University in central Colorado, where he obtained his Doctorate.

"Man, you scared me," he said, laughing.

"I said your name several times. You looked spaced out. Were you reading something? Did I interrupt?" she asked.

"No, nothing like that. Just going through some junk email. Guess I was concentrating more than I thought," he replied. He stood and walked over to her, giving her a quick peck on the cheek. She gave him a warm embrace.

"Want to walk down to the cafeteria and get some coffee?" he asked.

Patty looked confused. "Don't you have a class at ten? That's only ten minutes. Do we have time?"

Dylan looked at his watch and then at the clock on the wall. It was ten minutes to ten. He was dumbfounded.

"Wow, time really got away from me. I sat down a little after eight. I didn't…" His words trailed off. He knew he had not looked at emails very long. He did remember his vision beginning to blur, and that concerned him.

He shook his head. "Patty, I think I had a seizure."

"What? You looked fine. You weren't shaking or anything," she replied skeptically.

"No, when I was a kid I had absence seizures. You don't shake violently, your brain sort of 'locks up' for a while. I haven't had one since I was, like, thirteen."

"Are you sure?"

"Not one hundred percent, no. Absence seizures usually only last a few seconds for most people but as I recall mine would last longer. I just don't know. It was a long time ago." Dylan gathered his things for his class and stuffed them in his messenger bag. "I'll make an appointment with the doctor later today. I'm sure it's nothing."

"I'll walk with you," she offered.

As they walked across the small campus, Dylan explained how he had a dozen or so absence seizures as a kid. They weren't frequent, and had stopped altogether not long after he turned thirteen. His doctor had told his mother he would probably just grow out of it and he did. Or so he had thought. He told her they weren't really dangerous as most of the time they only lasted a few seconds, and the person having one usually didn't even realize it. But his often lasted much longer.

He reached his classroom and they parted with a quick hug. Patty walked back to her office, and Dylan began teaching his class. Astronomy 100 was the lowest level class he taught, and it was hard for him to concentrate at times, but he got through it.

An hour later, he walked back to his office. He had office hours during this part of the day but no one was waiting on him at the moment. He decided against going to the doctor for now since he wasn't completely sure he had even had a seizure. He decided to wait and see if it happened again. Besides, there was a lot of data to go over from the night before, and that was just the distraction he needed.

Over the next couple of hours, he ate his lunch at his desk and helped a few students with questions. He looked at some of the data but there was nothing ground breaking. He kept looking at the clock, though, just in case he had another seizure.

In the afternoon, his friend Rusty popped in to see him. Dr. Russell Carlson was hands-down the most over-educated and over-experienced professor at the college. He had multiple doctorates in Theology and Archeology, and had traveled all over the world. Dylan had never asked his age, but he knew he had to be pushing seventy.

"Everything OK, my friend?" He asked Dylan.

"Sure, Rusty. How about yourself?"

"I talked to Patty and she said you thought you might have had a seizure," he inquired with a raised eyebrow.

"Yeah, I think I blew it a bit out of proportion. I lost track of time reading emails and chalked it up to a seizure. Silly, really. I shouldn't have jumped to conclusions."

"Still, it's not like you to lose track of time. You and time are very close, no?" Rusty's slight Middle Eastern accent would often fade in and out. According to him, he spent a lot of summers in Israel growing up 'like a good Jew.' His family later converted to Christianity when he was an adult.

"Even I have my off days," Dylan replied, smiling.

"Well, if you are sure, that is good enough for me. You and Patty still coming over tonight?"

"Absolutely. Patty is excited to see all your newest antiques. She can't wait to 'nerd out' with you. Did you need help bringing in boxes?"

"No, I went to my storage shed last night and brought in a lot of new stuff. Most of it is Civil War-related, I think. I need to mark my boxes better. Anyway, she and I will have a blast looking through them."

Rusty had a vast collection of antiques he had collected from around the world. His home, not far from Dylan's, was stuffed with curiosities from many time frames and cultures. His storage shed apparently had even more. All Patty had to do was mention a historical event and Rusty would produce some sort of relic from that time period. The three had spent hours examining them. Since Patty was now focusing on the Civil War for her Doctorate, Rusty had promised to show her some antiques dating from that time.

"I'll expect you about six?" Rusty asked.

"You bet. Are you cooking or are we getting pizza?"

"I'm cooking. I've got a hankering for my sisters' lamb kabobs. Her bbq sauce is amazing! You guys are going to love it."

"I can't wait," Dylan beamed.

"Great, great. I'll see you guys later then," Rusty replied, leaving the doorway and heading down the hallway.

Dylan returned to his work. He tried to focus, but gave up and decided to call his mother. He hoped maybe she could fill in his memory about his seizures. He shut the door and took out his phone to call her.

"Dilly!" The voice gushed in obvious delight. Louise Mathis had called her son 'Dilly' since he was a baby. His father, also named Dylan, had died in a car accident when he and his sister were very young. The name 'Dylan' brought obvious pains of grief to his mother for many years after, so she rarely referred to him by it unless, of course, he was in trouble. Now it was just a habit.

"Hi, Mom," he said.

"What a delightful surprise! You already made your weekly call on Sunday. Is everything alright?" She was only halfway joking as Dylan was such a creature of habit, he tended to call his mother every Sunday at around two in the afternoon and they would speak for almost forty-five minutes each time.

"Not really, maybe, I don't know," Dylan admitted, almost embarrassed.

"Well, as long as you're sure," she laughed.

"You remember when I was a kid and had those seizures?"

There was silence for a few seconds. "Yeah, I do. Such a scary time. Why do you ask?"

"It's silly, but I think I might have had another one."

"That doesn't sound silly. What do you mean by might?"

"I was reading through emails and before I knew it over an hour had passed."

"Happens to me all the time, darling," Louise lamented.

"Not like this. I had only read a few emails and my eyes kinda went blurry and the next thing I know Patty is trying to get my attention."

"Oh, sounds suspicious. Have you seen a doctor?" She asked.

"No, it just happened this morning."

"If it were anyone else, I would write it off as no big deal. But you, Dilly, are the only one I know that looks at the clock on the wall AND his watch every five minutes. I can't remember you ever being late for anything. You simply never lose track of time. I would get checked out. It couldn't hurt."

"Maybe your right," he replied. "I just have very bad memories of all the tests they used to do to me."

"Well, what do you expect? You were a special case. Your seizures would last anywhere from a few seconds to an hour. None of the specialists had ever seen anything like that before. If they have returned, you need treatment."

Dylan thought for a minute. "When did they go away? I don't remember it as being a big deal. I just didn't have them anymore."

"The last one you had was a few weeks after you turned thirteen. I remember it because it was right before the worst morning of my life."

"I remember that," Dylan chimed in. "That guy was a jerk."

"Yes, he *was*," Louise agreed, her emphatic voice denoting the word 'jerk' not being strong enough for her.

After an awkward few seconds, Dylan asked, "Did I ever get tested again?"

"Nope, the doctor said it would likely happen, so we just let it go. After a few years with no seizures and no medication, you were officially seizure-free."

Dylan thought for a minute. "Well, I guess I'll call my doctor then. It can't hurt, right?"

"I think that would be wise, Dilly," Louise replied. She then switched trains of thought. "Are you going to be seeing your sister anytime soon?"

"I may be driving down to Fort Collins this weekend. That comic book store I like is downtown. I'll see if Melanie wants to have lunch. I'm sure she will since Patty will be with me. She talks to her more than me anyway."

"Well, Melanie never had a sister. She is really looking forward to you two getting married so it is official," she declared slyly.

"Let's not get ahead of ourselves," Dylan broke in, laughing.

"I know, I know," she said, interrupting.

"I'll call you again Sunday, Mom, unless I learn anything new."

"Alright, Dilly, I love you."

"Love you, too."

Dylan hung up and began searching for his doctor's number. Finding it, he called and made an appointment for early the next morning. According to his nurse, Doctor Hurst would give him a physical and an EEG. If needed, he would refer him to a specialist. 'Poking and prodding and brain zapping,' that's what his sister had called it when he was little. *Good times, good times,* he told himself.

***

Fifty miles south of Laramie, Sissy Friedmen is walking along Highway 226. She is carrying everything she owns in a large backpack on her back. While she normally loves walking, her long trek and lack of sleep is taking its toll. The terrain, even along the road, is rocky and treacherous. There were very few trees to block the never-ceasing Wyoming wind.

A sleek, black Mercedes approached from the south and slowed to a stop beside her. Sissy gazed at the black beauty before her, not seeing many luxury cars this far north of Denver. The window rolled down and the voice of an older gentleman spoke from the driver seat.

"Do you need a ride, my dear?" cooed the voice.

"I don't know, man, I'm pretty dirty," Sissy replied, leaning over on the side of the window.

"That's not a problem for me," the voice drawled calmly.

Sissy was hesitant, but tired. She looked at the man in the driver seat. Well-dressed, kind eyes, sweet smile and younger than his voice sounded.

"You can put your pack in the back seat. Sit there or in the front, your choice."

Sissy decided she could trust him for now and stowed her pack in the back seat and opened the front door, sitting in the comfy leather seats.

"My name is Sissy," she blurted, sticking her hand out.

"I'm Dag," the man replied, shaking her hand gently, but keeping his eyes on the road.

"You came along just in time. I didn't get much sleep last night, so I am dead on my feet."

"Are you from the area, Sissy?"

"I'm from Casper, but I've been living in Fort Collins for the last year. I decided yesterday it wasn't working out there, so I'm going home. I don't have a car, so I figured I could hike there in a week. It's a good time of year to hike. How about you?"

"Me? I'm from all over the place, but I've been in Colorado for a while now. I have business in Laramie, so that's why I came across you today." Dag smiled.

"I guess I lucked out. If you can take me to Laramie that will knock a day and half off my trip."

"Glad to help," Dag said. They drove in silence for a brief time. As they reached a small forested area, Dag spoke again.

"Tell me, Sissy, does your family know what you were doing in Fort Collins?"

"What do you mean?" Sissy replied.

"Do they know you were a prostitute and a drug addict?"

Sissy began shaking. "What makes you think that? Are you a cop?"

"No, nothing like that. You have the stink of drugs and dozens of men on your soul. And your eyes, so full of your many sins."

"Okay," Sissy gulped. "I think it's time for you to pull over and let me out." She was angry and scared and this 'holy roller' was giving her the creeps.

Dag began to slow the car. "Does your family know about the man you stabbed last night? He died, you know."

"You're crazy, man! Stop this car, now!"

"Absolutely," Dag said as he pulled off the deserted highway onto the side of the road. "I am starving...."

The high-pitched squeal coming from the car wasn't Sissy. She would never make another sound.

Chapter 2 – The Rabbit Hole

From the outside, Rusty's home looked like a normal two story Craftsman. It was large for his street, but every neighborhood in the area had at least one oversized house. Many of them had been reconfigured into tiny studio apartments to house the many university and junior college students in Laramie. Like most of the homes in the neighborhood, Rusty's house was over a hundred years old.

The inside of the house was a different story, every room decorated with a different historical theme. The living room was Victorian. The dining room ancient Egyptian. The kitchen Old West. These were the only rooms Dylan had seen so far, but Rusty assured him every room was unique.

Dylan and Patty arrived on time, bringing a bottle of Rusty's favorite wine. It was actually a very cheap brand but hard to find, and Rusty loved it for some reason. The aroma of grilled meat filled the house and, as they entered, Dylan's mouth began to water.

"That smells incredible!" Dylan marveled.

"I've never eaten lamb before, but if it tastes anything like it smells, I think I'm going to be having a lot more of it," Patty agreed.

"As I said, my sister's recipe. She was an incredible cook. The miracles she could work with any kind of meat and a few spices, well, she was an artist," Rusty sighed with a faraway look in his eyes.

Dylan noticed he spoke of her in the past tense, so he didn't ask any more about her.

"Hey, you brought my favorite wine!" Rusty stated.

"Yeah, the beauty of living in a college town. No shortage of liquor stores."

"Well, dinner is nearly finished. Have a seat in the dining room while I pour the wine."

"Are you sure we can't help?" Patty asked.

"Oh no, you are guests. Sit, I'll bring in the wine and the food shortly."

Dylan and Patty made their way to the dining room. While Rusty insisted much of the décor were reproductions, they were impressive none-the-less. Patty marveled at the carved tablets and obelisks. Dylan rubbed the metal and colored glass jewelry. There was a life-sized bronze cat in the middle of the table. Other than the modern lighting, you'd swear you were in ancient Egypt.

Rusty brought the wine in with three wooden goblets. They also appeared very old, and the interiors were slightly stained. Dylan didn't recognize the carvings on them.

"I've never seen these before, Rusty," Dylan declared.

"They have been in my family many years. You have never truly experienced wine until you have drunk from aged wooden cups. It adds flavor. Trust me, you will love it."

As Rusty poured the wine, Dylan noticed he had left a little water in his own cup. Rusty always watered down his wine. He said it reminded him of drinking wine as a kid. His parents allowed it, but only if he watered it down first. He got a taste for it and always watered down, even the most expensive brands.

Next, Rusty brought in the food. Dylan and Patty went on and on about how good it looked and smelled. Then they tasted it and went on some more. Patty asked questions about items in the room all through dinner and Rusty was happy to speak about them.

After dinner, Patty and Dylan insisted on cleaning the dishes. Rusty packed them a to-go bag and placed it in the refrigerator. He opened another bottle of wine then suggested they go to his work area in the basement.

The basement was unfinished and undecorated. The walls were cinderblock with a few high windows. There were half a dozen long tables filled with various stone and metal pieces. Tools for cleaning and restoration were sitting out, along with a few oil lamps and candles that had been used recently. Unlike the rest of the house, this room was all business.

"Wow, Rusty, I've never been down here before," Dylan said in amazement. "This is some workspace."

"I get artifacts from friends around the world from time to time. They like me to restore them or date them."

"What's with all the candles?" Patty inquired, picking up a small stone tablet.

"Many antiques are best viewed by candlelight. It's how many of them were created. I don't use them all the time, but I like to keep them out just in case. Of course, I have UV lights and infra-red lights, too. Even the ancients liked to hide things." Rusty pointed to a cabinet in the corner containing some very impressive looking equipment.

They walked along the rows of antiquities, taking it all in. Rusty chimed, "the Civil War table is on the far end near the window." They all moved in that direction. The basement was huge, spanning the footprint of the entire house.

As they reached the table, Rusty gently picked up a large rusty revolver. "This is a Colt 1851 Navy Revolver. Do you remember the Battle of Chancellorsville?"

"Yeah, 1863. It's where Stonewall Jackson was accidentally shot by his own troops."

"Exactly. This particular revolver belonged to Stonewall Jackson himself."

"Really?" Patty asked. "I thought his revolver was on display somewhere?"

"That is some frilly French gun given to him by his men. Very pretty, very reliable, but hard to get the ammunition for. This is the one he carried into battles." He placed it under a large illuminated magnifier. "See these markings? That is the proof stamp."

"Remarkable," Patty intoned slowly as she took the pistol and stared at it under the glass.

Dylan could see he was no longer a part of this conversation. As the two spoke intently, Dylan decided to explore some of the other artifacts. He moved slowly around the room, stopping to run his finger over something or read a tag now and them. There were so many things to look at. In the far corner, something caught his eye. It appeared to be a weathered, brass telescope.

He moved towards it, walking slowly between the tables. As he neared the telescope, he glanced to his side at what appeared to be a polished silver tray propped up on its side. He stopped to look at it as something in the reflection looked off. His reflection was distorted somehow, but the other things in the room weren't. However, it was darker in that part of the room, so he couldn't quite make out the image.

"The light is not very good over there," Rusty shouted. "There is a candle and a lighter nearby if you need to see something better." Rusty then turned back to continue speaking with Patty.

Dylan lit the candle and looked closer. The image was his, but somehow different. He looked at the reflection of other items on the table and they seemed fine, but not his. Something was off in his reflection. He blinked and moved his face, and the reflection did the same as expected. He opened his mouth and stuck out his tongue and so did the reflection. He stared at the eyes. Suddenly it hit him; they were a different color than his! His vision began to blur.

Patty was saying his name. He turned his head to look at her. She had a very worried look on her face.

"What's wrong, Patty?" he asked.

"Oh thank goodness!" she sighed. She hugged him tightly. "You've been zonked out for ten minutes! I've been shaking you and saying your name over and over!" She hugged him tighter.

Dylan looked around. Rusty was on his other side, looking equally concerned.

"Ten minutes?" he asked.

"That's just how long we've been aware of it," Patty replied. "I don't know how long you were over here before we realized it."

"Aw man, I had another seizure," Dylan grimaced.

"It was as if you were made of stone, my friend. Do you remember anything?" Rusty asked.

"I just remember looking at my reflection in this silver tray and then things went blurry." Dylan pointed to the tray on the table.

"It's a mirror," Rusty explained. "It's Egyptian and over five thousand years old. They didn't have glass mirrors back then, so the elite polished reflective metals and stone to see their reflections. I've polished this one for hours to get it to shine as well as it does."

"Do you feel alright?" Patty asked.

"Yeah, a little thirsty, though. And my knees feel achy from being locked."

"Have a seat. I'll get you some water," Rusty offered, hurrying up the stairs.

Patty led him over to where they were sitting. "I'm fine, Patty, really."

"I'm not sure I am. You looked like you were in a trance or something. You were completely still. When I ran over here, I didn't slow down fast enough and accidentally ran into you. I bounced right off. You didn't budge a bit. And you were mumbling incoherently. I was ready to call an ambulance."

"Mumbling?" Dylan asked.

"It sounded like gibberish, like you were babbling. Rusty recorded a little with his phone."

Rusty returned with a glass of water. "Rusty, let him hear the sounds he was making," Patty said.

Rusty took out his phone and played the sounds as Dylan took a long drink. It was monotone, like he was reciting something, but the words sounded like nothing Dylan had ever heard. After a few minutes, Dylan had heard enough. "You can turn it off. They aren't words. It's just my brain misfiring."

"That is what I was thinking," Patty agreed. "But it sounded like it had sentence structure or something. It was a little scary."

"Well, I feel fine now, but we should probably head home anyway. I've got a doctor's appointment in the morning, and Patty has to teach an eight o'clock class."

"Sure, sure, you can look at this stuff any time you want," he said to Patty. "Let me know if there is anything you would like to borrow. What good is history if we can't learn from it, no?"

"Thanks, Rusty. I'll definitely take you up on that," Patty replied as they walked up the stairs. On the porch, they said their goodbyes, then Dylan and Patty walked to her car and they drove away. Rusty watched and waved as they pulled away, then turned and dialed his phone as he walked into the house.

Patty drove the few short blocks to Dylan's house. They walked in together, Patty feeling right at home. They cuddled up on the couch and talked about the evening. Dylan loved just sitting in the dark with Patty with only the moon light to see by. It was peaceful.

They had been there for an hour or so when Patty decided it was time to go. She rarely stayed the night due to her strong religious beliefs, though Dylan himself had never been religious. He certainly respected her for strong beliefs and never pressured her for anything more than she could give. The few times she had stayed over were due to poor weather conditions, and even then they had slept in separate rooms.

At her car, they kissed goodnight and she drove off. Dylan took a deep breath of the crisp night air. He looked up at the cloudless sky, staring at the stars and marveling for the millionth time how infinite it all seemed. Since Laramie was at a high elevation, there was little air pollution to interfere with the view. It was magnificent, and Dylan found himself staring intently, peering from one star to the next.

He soon realized his feet were no longer touching the sidewalk. He looked down and saw he was about ten feet off the ground and rising slowly. He began to panic and reached out for something to grab hold of. There was a tree branch a few feet above his head and he grabbed at it. His vision began to blur.

The next morning Dylan woke with a start. He sat up in bed and looked around, befuddled. He assessed his surroundings. His alarm had gone off. He was in his bed and in his pajamas. Everything was as it should be. Except he didn't remember going to bed. He remembered…falling? Falling…up? Maybe it was floating. He also remembered the blurred vision again. Did he dream it? He got up and looked out the window into his front yard. Nothing was amiss. He walked outside and looked at the tree branch he thought he had grabbed. It looked undisturbed.

He walked back in the house, completely bewildered. He stumbled through his morning routine, doing things out of order and forgetting some steps altogether. He was shaken.

When ready, he decided to walk to the doctor's office. It was only five blocks and he felt like he needed it. The cool morning air really woke him up. He didn't realize how cold it was until he was halfway there. It was no more than forty-five degrees, and all he had on was a long-sleeved shirt. He decided to just keep going.

The doctor's office was thankfully very warm inside. He didn't wait long before being called into the back. He spoke with the nurse, recalling for her his neurological history, which they already had. He wasn't sure why doctor's offices did this, but they all did it, so it wasn't that weird. Then he sat and waited for the doctor.

Doctor Hurst soon came in and they exchanged pleasantries. They knew each other well due to the doctor's love of amateur astronomy. He had spent many evenings with Dylan and a group of local amateurs on the roof Dylan's office building, looking at the stars. After a brief discussion, he decided to do an EEG on Dylan right then. He had the nurse perform the test, which consisted of Dylan wearing a rubber cap on his head with some electrodes hooked to a machine. The machine recorded his brainwave pattern and printed it out for the doctor to analyze.

Within half an hour the results were ready for the doctor. He came in and looked them over. He excused himself and went looking for the nurse, and returned a few minutes later.

"Is there a problem, Doc?" Dylan asked.

31

"I'm not sure, Dylan. I did rotation in Neurological as a resident, and I've never seen anything like this."

"Of course, you haven't," Dylan remarked matter-of-factly.

"No, I'm serious. Your Theta and Delta Waves are huge. That normally only happens when you're asleep. There are some spikes which most likely confirm epileptic seizures, but these readings are weird."

"Exactly what you want to hear from your doctor," Dylan blurted out with a laugh.

"Listen, I'll give you a prescription for an anti-seizure medication for now, but I know a Neurological Specialist in Denver. He's great with this kind of thing. The weird stuff. And you're in luck because he owes me a big favor. I'll send him these results and see what he can make of it."

"What, did you save his life?" Dylan asked jokingly.

"No, I married his daughter and took her far enough away that she could visit often but not be over every day."

"You're a prince."

"Hah! Just wait until we have his grandchildren. I'll probably finally get written into the Will."

They both laughed and moved to the door. "Nancy will call your prescription in. Start it today and follow the dosage closely. I'll get some blood from you soon so we can monitor your liver function. That stuff can do a number on some people."

"Thanks, Doc. Will you be at the monthly meeting?"

"Absolutely. I never make plans for the last Saturday of the month, so I know I can be there."

They shook hands and Dylan left the building. He felt a little better getting medication, but the results certainly had him thinking.

How could his brain be asleep while he is awake? It made no sense to him, but he wasn't exactly an expert on brain activity.

To his surprise, Patty was waiting outside in her car. Her *warm* car, Dylan rejoiced. She told him she finished her class and decided to drop by to see if he needed a ride. She had only just gotten there and was going to call him as soon as she parked. They decided to go get some coffee and a donut while they waited for the prescription to be filled.

They drove to a chain coffee shop, ordered and took a seat at a table. They discussed his results and treatment. Patty was surprised, as well.

"Asleep? How can your brain be asleep? You're walking around, talking. It makes no sense."

"I know, it sounds crazy."

"Did they ever tell you that when they tested you as a kid?"

"Not that I remember, but I think we only ever visited our family doctor. He did run lots of tests, but he might not have been as schooled as Dr. Hurst. I think he diagnosed me more on what the symptoms were. Specialists were very expensive even then and I doubt Mom had the money. Our family doctor was a good guy and probably gave Mom a break on the costs."

"You've mentioned before you guys were very poor growing up. But you don't talk about it much."

"Not too much to talk about, really. My father died when I was ten. A car wreck, probably drinking and driving, since I remember him being drunk a lot. Mom worked as a waitress and went to school in the evening on and off. We lived in a cheap apartment complex. Eventually Mom got her degree in nursing and life got a little easier."

"When did you start having seizures?"

33

"Not long after Dad died. The doctor said the stress might have been a trigger." Dylan sipped his coffee.

"Are you stressed now? I mean, recently."

Dylan thought about it for a minute. "No, I would say my life is going very well. I have a great job doing that I love. I'm in love with a beautiful woman who seems pretty fond of me, too." Patty blushed. "I really have no problems I can think of."

They sat without speaking for a short time. Both were obviously very thoughtful.

"When did you stop having seizures?" Patty asked.

"It's funny. Mom and I talked about that the other day. Not long after I turned thirteen, they just stopped. I only had them sporadically anyway, but then I just didn't have them anymore. The doctor said I would probably grow out of it, and I thought I had."

"Is that when your mom got a better job? Maybe there was less stress."

"No, she still had another year or so before that happened. It may have had something to do with our neighbor."

"Your neighbor?"

"Yeah, he was an old guy named Stew. Retired salesman, I think. He was very grandfatherly towards us. At least when Mom was around. When she wasn't, he was a real jerk to me. Used to push me around, call me 'sissy,' punch me in the stomach, that sort of thing."

"Sounds like a peach. Did you tell your mom?"

"Nah, I couldn't. Sometimes she would work a double shift for extra money. Usually the overnight shift, then she could sleep while we were at school. We would spend the night at Stew's apartment. He wasn't that bad. And he never laid a hand on Melanie, or I would have said something." Dylan actually felt a pang of aggression in his stomach when he spoke of Stew and Melanie.

34

"So, if you said anything, your mom couldn't work? That's terrible, Dylan!" She took his hand into hers.

"It wasn't that bad. It didn't happen all that often. I could take a little punishment if it meant helping my mom."

"Did she find out eventually? Is that what relieved your stress?"

"No, not exactly. One night she left us with Stew and he had been drinking more than usual. He sent Melanie to bed early. He never let her see him hit me. He started with the verbal abuse and this time the physical abuse went too far. He punched me hard enough in the face that I passed out. When I woke up, he was gone. I had a huge shiner and a bloody nose. My ribs ached like crazy. I just waited there for hours for Mom to come."

Patty looked very distraught. "Where did the guy go?"

"No one knows. He never came back. The police looked for him and found nothing. They figured he ran off when he realized that he couldn't hide the abuse this time. He didn't take anything but his wallet so he couldn't be tracked easily. Mom felt terrible when she found out what he had been doing and never left us alone again. Pretty much smothered us after that. Who could blame her?"

"Your poor mom. I mean, poor you, but your mom. It must have been horrible for her learning the truth."

"Oh yeah, it changed her. She was always a loving mother, don't get me wrong, but after that she was driven. She never wanted to have to be dependent on anyone again. She worked hard, finished school, and got a better job in a doctor's office. She never missed a parent conference, or school program, or Science Fair. I know it was a strain on her physically, and mentally, but I think it helped her to focus more, too. Might have been the best thing to ever happen to us when you think about it."

They continued chatting for a while and left when they finished their coffee. Dylan's prescription was ready at the pharmacy and they picked it up and drove to work. Patty had another class to teach in the afternoon, and Dylan had data from the previous night to examine.

They parked, quickly kissed, and parted to their respective offices. Dylan took the medication as soon as he got back to office. Later, he ate his lunch at his desk and tutored a few of his students in Oort's Constants in the early afternoon.

That night, Dylan and Patty ate a quiet dinner at Dylan's house. They watched a movie together then sat outside and looked at the stars. As they snuggled on a bench, Dylan realized how happy he was. He hoped Patty could say the same. By ten o'clock, Patty was on her way home and Dylan was getting ready for bed.

The next morning, Dylan woke and began his normal routine. It wasn't until he was dressed and checking his weather instruments that he realized how great, how *normal* he felt. Maybe it was the medication he had begun taking, or just peace of mind from visiting the doctor, but he felt like his normal self again, odd habits and all.

He went to work, taught his morning class and had lunch at his desk. He delved deep into the data from the last couple of days, since he didn't spend much time the day prior. Most of all, he relished the normalcy.

Just after three o'clock, Rusty knocked on his open door. "You busy?" He asked.

"Not really. Just looking through some of this logged data from last night."

"Anything new?"

"Well, there may be a new comet impacting Jupiter in the next four years, but it looks like two other researchers have already named it." He sat back in his chair and put his hands behind his head. "Missed it by a week."

"Bummer," Rusty replied. "Maybe this will brighten your day. Do you have time to look at something?" He raised his hand from behind his back to show a very old looking book.

"Sure! Whatcha got?" Rusty handed the book to Dylan gently.

"Careful, it's very old."

Dylan took the book carefully and sat it on his desk. He opened it slowly, being careful not to overtax the binding. "This looks interesting," he mused.

"Have you ever heard of the Voynich Manuscript?"

Dylan thought for a moment. "That's that ancient book that no one understands, right?"

"Exactly. It's believed to have been written in the 1400's. At least that is what it has been carbon-dated to. No one knows the author but it was first brought to prominence by a book dealer named Voynich in the early 1900's. It does have several languages, including Latin, but there is one language no one has ever been able to decipher."

"Cool. Is this book somehow related to it?"

"Yes. The original book is mostly about herbs and alchemy, and a little astronomy based on what is written in Latin and the numerous pictures. It even contains a picture of a sunflower only found in the Americas, decades before Columbus 'sailed the ocean blue.' But, it has long been believed that the tome is missing many pages. Maybe even whole sections."

"Interesting," Dylan uttered, carefully thumbing through the book.

"Yes, it is. Especially because you are looking at the missing pages."

Dylan stopped turning the pages and carefully took his fingers off the book. He stared at it intently. "These pages are six-hundred years old? Where did you get it?"

"These have been in my collection for many years. I assume someone at some time removed them on purpose, because these pages have their own cover that is also very old. I had a chance to get my hands on the rest of the piece a few years back, but it got donated to Yale before I could act." Rusty noticed Dylan seemed hesitant to touch it. "You can touch it, it's okay."

Dylan rubbed his hands on his pants and resumed thumbing through it. Rusty continued, "these pages seem to deal with just astronomical phenomenon. The same languages appear, too. But it's the astronomy I have little knowledge of, so I brought it to you."

Dylan noted planet movement charts, some math dealing with gravity and even some drawings that looked like asteroids. It seemed familiar, but, of course, he understood very little of the writing.

"Whoever drew these was way ahead of their time. Most of this planetary movement data wouldn't be discovered until hundreds of years later."

"There is one particular illustration I would like you to see. It's near the back. A large circle with a bunch of geometric shapes filling it."

Dylan turned the pages until he saw it. "Here it is. It...it kind of looks like doodling, but there's order to it." Dylan stared intently at the image. His vision began to blur.

Chapter 3 – Illumination

Dylan awoke slowly. He was sitting in a room with low light. *A basement?* he thought. He focused on the area around him and realized he was tied to the chair he was sitting in. There were candles all around the room. He recognized it as Rusty's basement.

He tried to remember what happened. He was at work reading a book. No, an ancient book Rusty had brought him. He remembered looking at an image of a bunch of geometric lines, then the blurriness. And now he was here, tied to a chair in Rusty's basement!

"Rusty?" He queried, not as loudly as he wanted. His throat felt very dry. It felt like he had been lecturing all day. "Rusty!" he yelled much more loudly.

Rusty came down the stairs quickly. "Oh, great, you're awake!"

"Why am I tied up in your basement?!" Dylan asked.

"It was easier," Rusty replied.

"Easier than what?" Dylan asked.

"You wouldn't have believed me any other way." Rusty began to walk towards him. He was carrying a large knife.

Dylan eyed the knife and Rusty put it on the table next to him. "I have a lot to tell you, Dylan." He sat down in the seat directly across from him. "I'm sorry about the bindings, but experience tells me to leave you tied up until I'm done."

"Experience with what? Are you going to kill me? Sell my kidney?"

"Dylan, what I am going to tell you is going to shock you, and I can't have you running out of the house until you hear everything."

"Man, I thought you were eccentric, not crazy!"

"Oh, it gets worse, I promise, but everything I am going to tell you is the honest truth." Rusty had a very serious look on his face as he leaned in and stared into Dylan's eyes. "I know you are not religious, but have you read the Old Testament?"

"Like, the Bible?" Dylan asked.

"Yes, the Holy Bible."

"Just some Sunday School as a kid, and what I've picked up from Patty. What does this have to do with me being tied to a chair in your basement?"

"Do you believe in God?"

"What the heck kind of question is that? Are you going to arrange a meeting?" Dylan was starting to sweat. For a moment, he actually believed his friend was going to kill him.

"Please answer the question, Dylan. It's important."

"Okay, yes I believe there is a god of some kind. I don't know which representation, but something exists, yes. There is too much order in the universe not to be some grand design."

"Good, good, there is hope," Rusty said. "Now listen closely. In Genesis Chapter six, Moses wrote of angels taking human brides and the resulting children were referred to as Nephilim. These children were bigger, faster, stronger and smarter than regular humans. Some even had amazing abilities."

Dylan looked at Rusty incredulously. "Are you serious? You tied me up to give me a Bible lesson?"

"Please, listen, and keep an open mind. This took place before the Flood. In fact, you could say it caused The Flood. God was angry, which is a scary thought in itself. Angels were created to fulfill a specific purpose, to worship and serve the Father. Though our basic biology is the same, our DNA was never meant to mix. The children were mighty, as the Bible states, but their descendants were anything but. Human DNA was perfect from the moment of creation. We had extraordinarily long and healthy life-spans. When angelic DNA mingled with it, many of the genetic disorders you see today, things like Diabetes, Down's syndrome, Huntington's disease, they became part of our gene pool."

Dylan shook his head from side to side. "I'm not saying I'm buying into any if this, but why would God be mad at us? Why not be mad at the angels?"

Rusty's head sank. "The angels had it much worse. You know the story of Lucifer?"

"He's the Devil, right?"

"Exactly. The Book of the Revelations of John speaks of a War in Heaven and Lucifer and other angels being cast out of Heaven, becoming what we traditionally call the Devil and his demons. This took place around the same time Man was created. Lucifer and others refused to serve God by helping Man. There wasn't a War in the traditional sense. Michael and the other angels killed their physical bodies. When the physical form of Man or angels die, their spiritual forms go to the Realm of the Dead, called Sheol. At least, that is what the Hebrew word is. This is an entirely different plane of existence. The righteous then travel to a paradise called Heaven."

Rusty got a faraway look in his eye as he spoke. Dylan could see he had some personal connection to what he spoke of. "So, the unrighteous go to Hell?" Dylan asked.

"Yes. As I understand it, it's not a great place to be. Lots of pain and torment as you are forced to feel your regret. The burning comes later, at the end of it all. Since The Fallen, that's their preferred moniker, were cast out, the only place they could go was Hell. Lucifer, who was indeed special among the angels, naturally assumed control."

"All of this is in the Bible?" Dylan asked.

"Most of it. Other information I have pieced together over the years from other…sources."

"So, what does this have to do with Nephilim?"

"I'm getting to that, but I had to make sure you understood the seriousness of angels defying the Father. Those angels that took human wives were cast out, as well. Killed by the Archangels, their spirits sent to Hell."

"Wow, harsh."

"He has rules. If we break them, we suffer the consequences. Same goes for divine beings, only more so. "

"Can they be forgiven, like us?"

"It's not the same. They are higher beings than us. We sin because we are overcome with temptation. They don't feel temptation like we do. They are more informed, more evolved mentally, if you will. They are not sorry for anything they do, which is what the root of forgiveness is."

"OK. Well, what happened to the Nephilim?"

"The Flood happened. The Father was angry and hurt by what had taken place. He decided to start over by washing the Earth clean of all life. But He found favor in Noah. He must have been an extraordinary human being for God to save only him and his family. You know the story, I'm sure. He had Noah build an ark to save his family and two of every animal. They lived. Everyone else, including

43

the Nephilim, were killed. But some of Noah's family already carried DNA of The Fallen, so their DNA remained in our gene pool. Our species would continue, but never be the same."

"I don't understand. What's the point of allowing our lives to be shortened?"

"I can't speak for God, but my guess would be to cut down on the wickedness. An evil person can do a lot of evil things in a thousand years. Sure, they could do a lot of good, too, but evil seems to spread so much faster. If an evil person, like Genghis Khan or Hitler lives only sixty or seventy years, the world can recover, even learn from the experience. After The Flood, according to the Word, He ended our time on this planet at a hundred and twenty years."

"But very few people have lived a hundred and twenty years."

"My guess is our gene pool has become too polluted. Along with the angelic DNA we were never supposed to possess, we have had thousands of years of mutations. One of my degrees is in molecular biology. Years ago, I was part of a group trying to understand the aging process, when we came across structures on chromosomes called telomeres. Telomeres shorten slightly every time the cell divide. Eventually, they get so short, the chromosome can no longer divide. This is most likely why our bodies wear out. It's widely suspected that cloned animals created from adult cells have shorter life spans because of this."

Dylan thought for a minute. "I knew about your two PhD's in Archaeology and Middle Eastern Studies. You have others?"

Rusty laughed and looked away. "Dylan, I have more degrees than I can remember, some from Universities that don't even exist anymore." He stood and walked over to a box.

"How is that even possible? I mean, you've obviously been around awhile, but you're not THAT old?"

Rusty found what he was looking for and brought it closer to Dylan so he could read it. It was a framed Diploma. Dylan read the banner across the top.

"Is that Latin? Universitas Harvardiana. Harvard University?"

"Yes. Now look at the roman numerals."

"MCMXV. 1915, I think."

"Look at the name."

"Russell Carlson. Your grandfather?"

"No, Dylan that was me. That is the oldest diploma I still have that is not stamped in metal."

Dylan was dumbfounded. "You would have to be over a hundred years old. That's not possible..." Dylan's voice trailed off.

"I am far older than a hundred years, truth be told, but just how old I cannot say. Let's just say I've been alive for many hundreds of years, and have learned a few things." He motioned with both hands in a large circle. "And I have collected many things, as well."

Dylan was silent. He must have been contorting his face pretty hard because Rusty noticed. "It is not an easy thing to comprehend, my friend. I would love to go into it further, but there are rules pertaining to what I can and cannot reveal. Rules I've chosen to live by for most of my long life."

"Are you one of The Fallen?" Dylan asked.

"Heavens no," Rusty replied with a laugh. "But in my life, I have met a few. And I have met a few like you, as well."

"Like me?"

"Yes, you are far rarer than mere angels, my friend."

Dylan shifted in his chair. He had forgotten for a moment that he was tied up. He looked Rusty in the eye. "Well, what am I?"

"It's not easy to explain. How much do you remember about genetics? Mendel and all that?"

"Not much. Biology never really interested me."

"Do you remember the concept of dominant and recessive genes? You know that human DNA is organized into genes and they are packed into forty-six chromosomes, half from each parent?"

"Yeah."

"Good. The angelic DNA that survived in Noah's family was significant. Between them, there were chromosomes from many different types of angels. Remember that all humans currently on the planet descended from this one family. Over the next centuries, there was inbreeding and crossbreeding until the population grew large again. People traveled, created new villages and colonies. The angelic DNA was now dispersed around the entire cradle of civilization. Some had a lot of it, some had none. And still it is today, indistinguishable from human DNA for the time being."

"That's not possible," Dylan explained. "It's been shown conclusively that our population could not descend from three couples. I remember a lecture about it as an undergrad. Not enough diversity or something like that."

"Conclusively? I don't think most people can even begin to understand what that word means. The same type of scientists that say it could not happen, say that all humans are related. That we did not spring up from primates in different parts of the world, but from one person. They call her Mitochondrial Eve because they hypothesized her existence by examining mitochondrial DNA, which changes very little as it passes from mother to child. So how can one group of scientists say it is mathematically impossible for the entire human population to descend from three couples, and another group of scientists say all human life descended from a single female parent? Because they don't understand what the word 'conclusively' means.

46

When all else fails, look at the DNA. It never lies despite what lawyers might have you think."

Dylan thought about it for a moment. "I guess that makes sense. I've heard of the concept of Mitochondrial Eve."

"There are billions of people on the planet, and many of them contain whole chromosomes that came from The Fallen. Some possess just a few fragments of DNA. When either enough angelic genes or their specific chromosomes, I'm not sure which, are present in a person, The Fallen can dwell in their bodies. They aren't Nephililm, mind you, that would require half of their DNA be angelic in origin and for that to happen naturally would be quite impossible these days. These people are Vessels for spiritual beings."

"Spiritual beings?"

"The Fallen have no physical bodies. They reside in Hell unless they find a human body to indwell. The first few hundred years after the Flood, people like you were more common. Now, I know of less than a dozen around the world."

"So, you are saying I have one of The Fallen inside me?"

"Yes, I know you do."

"How can you be so sure?"

"Lots of reasons. For one, I can feel it."

"That's creepy."

"No, entities with a higher sense of spirituality can sense when others like us are near. I've had a lot of years to perfect it and I'm rarely wrong. I knew you were special the first time we met at the faculty mixer. You've probably felt it with me, too, you just didn't understand what it was."

Dylan thought about when he first met Rusty. He remembered Rusty gave him 'the creeps' at first, like he was hiding something. He figured he should have gone with his first instinct and he might not be tied up in a basement now.

"Another indicator was your blackouts. Too long to be traditional absence seizures and if your mom had taken you to a specialist, they would have told her that. Sometimes when the entity is trying to make contact with you, the Vessel goes into a trance-like state as he calls to your mind, and your mind tries to answer. It kind of locks up your brain for a time. For how long depends on how badly they want to make contact. Since the entity can see what you see, they never try and make contact while you are doing something dangerous, like driving or climbing a mountain. If their Vessel dies, they go back to Hell."

"Is it possible for me to communicate with him? I mean, if he keeps trying, it must be possible."

"That is why we are here, my friend. We have been speaking with your guest for the last hour."

Dylan was stunned. *Could all this be true?* he thought. It all seemed silly, but he knew there was something to it. Then a thought occurred to him.

"You said 'we have been talking.' I only see you and me."

A voice came from the shadows as Patty stepped forward and revealed, "I'm here, too, Dylan." She gave him a faint but concerned smile.

"She helped me to bring you here, Dylan. The image you looked at from the Voynich Manuscript was an ancient pictograph that allows the Fallen to come forward for a short time with no ill effects, but it leaves the body very weak. I had to help you walk. Patty happened by as we were leaving and I explained what was happening as best I could. She was understandably skeptical, but she helped me get you down here so we could speak to him in private."

"Is all this true, Patty? Is there something, someone inside my head?"

"Yes, Dylan, I am convinced of it."

"And you both spoke with him?"

"Yes," Patty replied. "In fact, it was his idea to tie you to the chair. He knows you very well."

Dylan turned to Rusty. "Can I speak with him?"

"That's what we are going to try now. There is a silver tray on the table next to you. When a Vessel looks into shiny silver, the reflection they see is not their own, but their guest. It looks like them, but it is not. This allows you to see him with your eyes and hear him with your ears. Shall we proceed?"

Dylan still wasn't sure what to think. This made no sense to him, but he wanted to know for sure. "Let's do it," Dylan said.

Rusty set the silver tray up on its side by laying it against several books. He took out a small rag and wiped the tray in small circles, shining it up again. Dylan looked at his reflection and it seemed unremarkable. He stared further and noticed an odd difference in the eyes as they stared back at him. They weren't his eyes.

"Hello, Dylan," came a voice. Dylan realized his mouth was moving, but it did not sound like his voice. It was slower and deeper. Still, he recognized that it had come from his mouth.

"Hello," Dylan meekly greeted.

"I have waited many years to speak with you," the voice responded.

"This is very creepy," Dylan admitted out loud but to no one in particular. "What do I call you?" he asked.

"My name is Hydogall. Some have referred to me simply as Hyde if you prefer. I know humans like to shorten names."

"As in, Jekyll and Hyde?" Dylan laughed.

"Exactly, but his name was not really Jekyll."

"Are you serious? That was real? That was you?"

"I'm afraid so," Hydogall admitted. The face in the reflection turned serious and looked down.

"That's amazing," Dylan marveled.

"Even more importantly, the Vessel I moved to after him was Thaddeus Cray, an ancestor of yours. I've been traveling with your family ever since."

"This is just outrageous. I feel my mouth moving but it's not my voice. I see my reflection, but it's not mine exactly." Dylan began to shake more than before.

"Please, Dylan, calm down. I know this is scary, but believe me when I say that I am a part of you. I have been with you since your father died. It is as if we are the same person." Hydogall was almost pleading, his concern for Dylan obvious.

"You knew my dad?"

"Your father was my Vessel also. When he died, I moved to you."

Dylan thought for a minute and began to ask a question but Hydogall jumped in first.

"Yes, Dylan, he was inebriated when he crashed. He did not suffer much but his final words were of regret. Regret for what he had and had not done for you, your sister and mother. He was…regretful. As was I."

"You, what did you regret?"

"I did not interact with your father. I was content to watch and to feel like a living being. But my entry into you was premature. You were very young and that is what caused your seizures. Usually, we only enter adults, but I had no other choice."

"Then why did my seizures stop? Did I become an adult?"

"That was part of it, but not entirely. The main reason is a far more grave and I do not wish to upset you. Remember, I know you very well. You will blame yourself when the blame is completely on my shoulders."

"Blame? For what?" Dylan asked, suspiciously.

Chapter 4 – Dark Times

"The night Stew left you and Melanie alone. How well do you remember it?" Hydogall asked.

"Not very. I just remember Stew beating on me and then he was gone."

"I had such respect for you, Dylan. Not telling your mother because you knew she could not work extra without a free babysitter. But you were foolish."

"Well, yeah, I know that now," Dylan remarked to the mirror.

"Stew had imbibed more than usual. He knew when he hit you in the face that it was over for him. He knew he would go to jail. So, he decided if he was going to go away, he was going to make it worth it. He stared at your lifeless form lying on the floor and began walking towards the room where Melanie was sleeping. He had an unsettling smile on his face. I decided I could not let anything happen to her. She was so innocent and pure. So, with great difficulty and because you were unconscious, I took control. I grabbed Stew from behind and broke his arm. He spun around and I slapped him hard enough to break his jaw. I wrapped my hand around his throat, collapsing his trachea. He was still alive as I dragged him through the front door and flew high into the air, holding him by one foot. At two hundred feet above the town dump, I dropped him. He hit with such force, it buried his body completely. It seemed fitting for him to lie at the bottom of a pile of refuse. Then I returned to the apartment and lay down. You awoke hours later."

Dylan's mouth was dry and his brow was sweating. He was trying to process what Hydogall had just said. "You seem so nonchalant about it. You killed a man, so violently."

"I was an angel, Dylan. We were often the vengeful hand of the Father. And there was a personal connection. You love your sister. I love your sister, like a father and a brother. Stew deserved what happened to him, for what he did to you and for what he was about to do to Melanie. The world is a better place without him. Unfortunately, taking control of a Vessel without consent is extremely draining. I was, for lack of a better term, dormant for several months. I could still see and hear and feel everything you did, but I could not act or contact you. When I was no longer dormant, I was content again to just experience your life." The image in the tray turned towards Rusty. "You may untie him, now. He will not be running away."

Rusty untied Dylan who rubbed his teary eyes. He stood and walked around the open floor, pacing. Patty moved toward him and they embraced.

"Are you OK?" she asked.

"I don't know. There are so many questions."

"Dylan, I have known a few Vessels in my time. It's not easy for any of them when they find out. In the old days, it was a little easier, but now, in our pessimistic and non-spiritual society, it is even harder to accept. Take a moment. Process it. But know that Patty and I have been talking to Hydogall for a while. I don't believe he is evil. I think his words are genuine. I've been told angels, even The Fallen, are incapable of lying, but I'm not sure. It was one of them that told me that."

Dylan chuckled lightly. He walked back over to the chair and sat, staring at the mirror. "I have a lot of questions, but I need to know one thing first. Why now? Why are you trying to contact me now? After all these years?"

"There is a very good reason, Dylan, and I am afraid it is not good. You have not been paying much attention to the news, but I have. Something dangerous is coming. There have been several news reports lately about people, women mostly, being killed and their hearts removed. I would wager there are many more that have not yet been found. I have seen this type of thing before."

Patty chimed in. "I've been following this. The first body was in Oklahoma. An older woman addicted to meth. They thought she ran afoul of drug dealers or something. The next two were in Colorado. Both prostitutes, I believe."

"Exactly Patty. May I call you Patty?"

"Please do, Mr. Hydogall."

"Just Hydogall, if you please," he said smiling. "If you draw a line from the first body to the last, he is heading this way."

"Who?" Dylan and Patty asked in unison.

"Another Vessel, but this one is inhabited by a very evil entity. A former Angel of Death named Dagnem. He is sadistic and cruel. Oddly enough, I helped Thaddeus Cray kill his Vessel many years ago. I do not know what his given name was but the locals called him Jack."

"Jack the Ripper was inhabited by one of The Fallen?" Rusty asked. "I did not know this."

"Yes, for Dagnem, it was better than Heaven. To enter a being of such evil and be able to indulge his own sick desires was a dream come true. Thaddeus was a lawyer. After The Ripper killed his beloved, he was able to kill him. He did not require the use of any of my Spiritual Gifts."

"What gifts?" Dylan asked.

"Well, my particular Order of angels are called Watchers. And that is what we do. We watch and record mankind. We have the gifts of flight and invisibility. It helps in our duties. And of course, we are stronger than humans, more like five or six humans. I could not lift a car, but I could pick up one side."

"And I could do that, too?"

"Yes, with practice. You actually began to fly a few nights ago, but I stopped you. You were not ready for it."

"So that's what happened! And this Dagnem, he knows about…us?"

"The Fallen can sense each other from hundreds of miles away. You cannot pinpoint it, but you know which direction they are, and roughly how far. He is in Laramie now, but I cannot tell where. He is very dangerous, especially to us. He knows it was I that killed his Vessel and sent him back to Hell. He will want revenge, but he is patient. He knows I am in the area, but not where. He will probably begin killing locals until I show myself."

"Not to sound callous," Patty said, "but maybe you should just leave. Wouldn't that make him go?"

Rusty answered before Hydogall could. "Hydogall cannot simply leave unless another Vessel is nearby. Otherwise, he would return to Hell."

"Yikes, I'm sorry I asked," Patty moaned.

"I could leave," Dylan added.

"He would simply follow," Hydogall replied. "I am afraid you are going to have to face him. I am so sorry to put you through this, Dylan."

"Well, it sounds like you did the right thing, Hydogall. If you hadn't inhabited me, someone else, someone worse, might have."

"But you, my friend, have something he does not," Rusty said.

"What's that?" Dylan asked.

"Friends," Rusty smiled.

***

The Vessel inhabited by Dagnem walked around downtown Laramie. It was a small town, so it didn't take much time to cover every street. The buildings appeared very old with lots of brick. There were a lot of alleyways, which he liked. There would be many shadows there at night for him to hide in. And quite a few bars for him to find potential prey. The railroad yard that cut through the town would offer more anonymous fare for his delight. He smiled, thinking he could operate for many months in this town before suspicions arose. Plenty of time for him to find his main course. *And oh how he would make him suffer.*

***

"Why does this guy hate you, Hydogall?" Patty asked. "Wouldn't Hell be a paradise for The Fallen?"

Hydogall shook his head from side to side. "Hell is not pleasurable for anyone. It is the only place in all of Creation where The Father has no presence. You know nothing different on this plane of existence. It is a common belief that Hell is on fire. Trust me; Hell is a barren, cold place with not a shred of love or compassion. It is torment, even for the most evil of creatures. The closest thing I can compare it to is drowning without dying. Even Lucifer himself hates it there, although he tries to say different."

"How do you leave Hell?" Dylan asked.

"The Fallen may leave for a few minutes at a time but will be pulled back quickly without an anchor, a Vessel. Regular people that have not been baptized can act as short term Vessels, maybe an hour or two, but they are more like bus stops than vacations. You can also leave Hell long-term if you are invited to inhabit a body. Lucifer gets lots of invitations, so he is here constantly. Since most people do not know our names, we are not invited and must stay in Hell nearly all of the time."

"That's sad," Patty lamented.

"It seems that way, but remember that everyone in Hell has earned their place there. Even The Fallen," Hydogall said.

"Even you?" Dylan asked.

"Even me," Hydogall replied.

"But you seem so nice," Patty stated.

"I like to think I am. Nice has nothing to do with it. Well, it has a little to do with it, but I do not wish to speak of my transgression now, if you do not mind."

"No problem," Dylan declared. "Take your time."

Rusty spoke up. "Hydogall, we need to prepare Dylan for the battle coming to him. Is there any way you can speak to him without the mirror?"

"Yes, the reflection allows him and you to see me speak, but it is the silver that allows him to hear me. That is how I communicated with past Vessels, although I stopped doing so after Thaddeus Cray. It can be a bit…unsettling at first. As you now know well."

"I have a silver wristband," Rusty blurted. "It belonged to Lt. Colonel George Armstrong Custer. He was a very flashy guy." Rusty walked over to a box and fished through it until he found what he was looking for. He returned to Dylan and put it on his wrist.

"Let's hope it's a better good luck charm for us," Dylan lamented.

"We'll go out to my backyard. I think we can all use some fresh air. You can try some of your gifts. Hydogall will talk you through it."

The three walked up the stairs to the kitchen and out the back door. Dylan hadn't realized it was evening already. He looked at his watch and saw it was after eight. No wonder he was hungry, he thought. They walked into the middle of the backyard and looked around. The mature trees all around the property made it seem like they were miles away from anyone even though the house next door was within throwing distance.

"Okay, Hydogall, are you there?" Dylan asked looking around.

"I am always here, Dylan."

"Creepy!" Patty exclaimed.

"What?"

"Your mouth is moving, but the voice is different. I guess it wasn't so noticeable in the basement because we were all looking at the reflection. And when we were talking to Hydogall earlier, the voice didn't seem so different."

"I guess I have to get used to someone being in my head," Dylan stated.

"Let us try becoming invisible," Hydogall suggested. "Keep in mind that in order to use my spiritual gifts, I have to allow it. The other night, when you flew, I was as caught up in the vision of the heavens as much as you were. I relaxed a bit more than usual and that is why you began to rise. Luckily, you were only off the ground for a few seconds and I was able to stop it by causing a blackout. Then I guided you back into the house and into bed. Since it was only a few minutes, it did not take too much energy."

"How do I begin?" Dylan asked.

"Just imagine yourself fading away."

"OK," Dylan said. He closed his eyes and imagined his body fading away. He then opened his eyes. "Did it work? Can you see me?"

"Look at your hand," Hydogall pointed out.

"You look like a ghost!" Patty marveled.

Dylan looked at his hand and could still see it. However, his hand was very faint. He could see through it, but just barely.

"Concentrate, Dylan. Imagine your hand fading away until it is not there," Hydogall spoke slowly.

Dylan stared at his hand and it slowly faded away to nothing. He looked down and could no longer see his body. The only trace he could see of himself was the footprints he was leaving in the grass.

"Great job, Dylan! Now walk around the yard a bit. Get used to being invisible. It is not as easy as you think. With practice, it will become second nature."

Dylan walked around the large yard and onto the sidewalk. He stumbled several times, forgetting where his feet where, but he got the hang of it. He even jogged a little bit as he moved back to where Rusty and Patty were. As he reached them, he suddenly reappeared.

"Whoa!" Patty exclaimed. "You scared me! I didn't realize you were there."

"I guess I know how to turn it off," Dylan said. "It's like holding your breath while you're invisible then releasing it to become visible."

"Indeed," Hydogall concurred. "In time, you will be able to stay invisible for hours. Let us try strength next."

"I'm not very strong, I'm afraid."

"That is because I have not let you use *my* strength. And you will need to practice. Accessing that kind of strength is not easy. Your mind cannot comprehend it at first and it limits you. You must push past that limit."

Dylan walked over to a large cement urn holding a plant. It looked like it might weigh at least three-hundred pounds, well above what Dylan could normally lift.

"Is this important?" Dylan asked. "I don't want to possibly wreck something that came from ancient Greece."

"No," Rusty replied. "I bought it last year at a yard sale down the street. It took three young men to carry it back here, and that was when it was empty."

Dylan bent and grabbed around the base.

"Lift with your legs," Patty offered.

Dylan nodded and tried to pick it up. He felt it budge a little. He relaxed and tried again, this time it came off the ground a foot before slamming back down. He tried a third time, picking it up fully. He sat it back down gently.

"Wow! It wasn't easy, but once I got it up to my chest it felt more like fifty or sixty pounds than three-hundred."

"You will still need to work on it," Hydogall instructed. "Raw lifting is one thing. Knowing your limits with precision is another. It takes young children years to learn how to throw and catch with precision. You will need to test your limits in the coming days."

"True," Patty said. "You'll need to know how fast you can run or jump, or even punch if you're going to be fighting this thing."

"I hadn't thought of that," Dylan lamented. "I've never even been in a fight. I wouldn't know how to begin."

"Never?" Rusty asked.

"Never," Hydogall stated. "Since I have known him he has never once needed to fight. But do not worry; I have battled for much of my life, physically and spiritually. And I am sure Rusty has picked up a few things in his life."

"Mostly Krav Maga, a kind of Jewish Kung Fu. Trust me, it is very effective." Rusty assumed a typical Kung Fu pose.

Hydogall continued, "Well, I saved the best for last. Flying is the most exhilarating experience imaginable. I forgot how much I missed it until your demonstration the other night."

"Will I have wings?" Dylan asked, only half kidding.

"No, angels do not actually have wings. Most appear to be human. The wing concept came about because people that saw real angels flying could not comprehend it. The idea of a person flying through the air was so foreign to their minds that many just imagined they had wings to make it fit their memory better."

Dylan walked over to the middle of the lawn. The sun was down now and the evening was brisk. "What do I do?"

"The other night, you were staring up at the stars. As you did so, you probably imagined yourself among them. That is likely what began your ascent. When you fly, all that you are doing is controlling where your body is. You do not need to run or jump as in the cinema. You just imagine yourself rising and it happens. Imagine yourself moving forward or backward and that is what you do. Eventually, it will be second nature."

"You've said that about everything," Dylan stressed.

"It just takes time and practice. I do not know how much time we have, so we need to make the most of it."

"Okay, Okay, let's try." Dylan closed his eyes. "I'm imagining myself above the ground a few feet."

Patty gasped. "It's working!" she exclaimed.

Dylan opened his eyes and saw he was indeed a few feet off the ground. He wiggled his feet. "I didn't think it would be that easy." He paused. "I don't feel like I'm suspended from anything. It's not like I'm hanging from something. It's too weird." Dylan dropped to the ground suddenly. He was visibly shaken.

"You were doing well," Rusty encouraged.

"I don't like it. It feels…unnatural. I think I might be sick."

"The first time is the most disorienting," Hydogall said. "Next time will be easier, I promise."

Dylan sat down on the concrete planter. He rubbed his head, his body shivering intermittently. "You keep saying that. I'm sure it's true, but it's hard to imagine." Patty sat beside him and put her arm around his shoulders. She squeezed him tightly.

"A week ago, you were just an Astronomy professor," Rusty explained. "A few days ago, you became an Astronomy professor with a seizure disorder. That is hard enough to deal with. Now you are an Astronomy professor with a Fallen Angel inhabiting his body. No one expects this to be easy for you." Rusty's words were kind and supportive. "Nevertheless, there is a monstrously evil presence in Laramie, Wyoming. While it ultimately wants you dead, it will kill many others first. You are the only one that can stop it. With our help, of course."

There was a short lull in the conversation and then Patty spoke up. "I think he's done enough for one night. I want to get him home. He needs to rest."

"Yes, of course," Rusty agreed. "We can start again tomorrow. We'll have to wait until dark for flying lessons, but we can work on your strength and invisibility."

"Sounds good," Dylan affirmed half-heartedly. He started to remove the silver wristband and Rusty stopped him.

"Keep it, my friend."

"Rusty, I couldn't. It's a piece of history."

"It does more good now than it did for Custer. I only took it off his wrist so the other members of the tribes wouldn't be suspicious of me."

"You were there? You were an Indian, a Native American?" Patty asked.

"Yeah, but I lost my zest for it after Little Big Horn. The Calvary had been doing horrible things to the indigenous people and they were only returning the favor. There were no good guys left for me to side with."

The two stood and walked around through the side gate. They got in Patty's car and she drove him home. They went into his house together and Patty checked to make sure he was Okay. They kissed and she walked towards the door and stopped.

"So, every time I kiss you Hydogall experiences it?"

"Yes," Hydogall replied.

"That's weird," she said.

"I am sorry," Hydogall replied. "Humans are not meant to know about us for this very reason."

"It will be hard to get used to."

"I'm still the same man, Patty," Dylan avowed. It wasn't lost on him that he and Hydogall spoke with the same mouth. "The same man that still loves you."

She smiled weakly and walked out the door. Dylan turned, walked over to his recliner and sat down in the dark. He reached over to the curtain and pulled it back, looking out at the bright night sky.

"Hey, Hydogall?" he asked.

"Yes, Dylan?"

"You're ancient, right?"

"You could definitely say that."

"When you've revealed yourself in the past, did any of the people have spouses?"

"Yes, in the old days, they usually did."

"Did they stay together after they knew…about you?"

"Most often the Vessel did not tell their significant other. It is easier that way. Not once did telling the spouse work out, I am sorry to say. I know what Patty means to you and I deeply regret what is happening. If lives were not at stake, I would not have come forward."

Dylan sighed. "It's not your fault."

"It is, Dylan. I wish I could just leave, but I cannot."

The two were silent for a few minutes. Dylan then got up and got ready for bed. He performed his usual routine and in less than twenty minutes he was lying in bed.

Sleep didn't come quickly. Dylan stared at the ceiling for what seemed like hours. Then he imagined himself moving up to the ceiling and he began to rise slowly. He was aware of his movement and it rattled him a bit, but he kept going. He straightened up and began to move forward, floating through the house slowly.

"How'm I doin?" he asked.

"You are a natural, Dylan," Hydogall replied.

Dylan continued to move slowly around the house, into and out of each room, then back to his bedroom. He moved back down to the bed slowly. He breathed easier now, but soon realized he was covered in sweat.

"It was easier this time," he commented. "Not as unsettling."

"Baby steps," Hydogall replied.

After a few minutes of reflection, Dylan spoke. "Could you tell me about Jekyll? The real guy, I mean?"

"I suppose it was just a matter of time before you asked. Yes, I will tell you about him. And I will tell you about the final spiritual gift I have to bestow. Though 'gift' is not a word I like to use for it."

Chapter 5 – The Strange Case of Dr. Galion

London 1870

Dr. Paul Galion stared at the shelf containing a multitude of chemical bottles until he found what he was looking for. "Ah, silver nitrate, there you are," he declared in a jovial manner. He had been working on a medicine to cure infection for months now, and he was convinced some tincture of silver would be the answer. After all, the ancients used silver often for medicinal purposes. At least that is what his 'lab assistant' had told him.

Hydogall had revealed himself to Dr. Galion several months earlier in an effort to help him with his medical research. Finding a treatment for common infections, often proving fatal at the time, would save thousands of lives each year in Europe alone. Hydogall believed that perhaps his experience could help the good doctor.

Dr. Galion walked over to the polished silver serving tray and looked into it. "What do you think, my good man? Silver nitrate may be the key, eh?"

"You would know better than I, Dr. Galion," Hydogall replied.

Dr. Galion chuckled and moved to his lab station to prepare his new tincture. He worked for nearly an hour in silence, mixing the various chemicals, and making copious notes.

A knock at the door broke his trance-like state. An angry, irritated look developed on his face, but it faded as he calmed himself near the door. Dr. Galion's small bursts of anger had concerned Hydogall at first, but he always recovered his composure quickly. He was driven in his work, and that work would benefit all mankind.

He opened the door and found his good friend Thaddeus Cray. Thaddeus was a lawyer who often handled Dr. Galion's affairs.

They had met several years ago at a symphony, and bonded over their shared love of Chopin.

"Thad!" Dr. Galion exclaimed. "What brings you to my humble laboratory?" The two embraced as good friends do.

"I had to come quickly! I was seeing a client at the workhouse infirmary, and found there an elderly woman dying of sepsis in the room next door. I thought she might be a candidate for your treatment."

"I just mixed up a new batch, but I haven't had a chance to try it on the mice yet. I don't think we should move straight on to a grown woman."

"She only has a day or two left, Paul. Without a miracle, she will die. Is it not a moral imperative that we at least try to do something?"

A faint smile formed on Dr. Galion's lips. "Well, if she is going to expire anyway, I suppose we must try. Does she have family?"

"None to speak of. And I spoke with her and she is willing to try anything."

"Then we must hurry!"

Dr. Galion gathered his things and two left the lab and hurriedly walked the two blocks to the infirmary. The streets were cluttered with people and carts selling their wares. The infirmary was on the third floor of the workhouse, and when they reached the stairs, they found their way blocked by people sitting on the stairs. By the time they reached the correct floor, more than an hour had passed.

Hydogall tried to contact Dr. Galion, but since he wore no silver, he could not. He was worried about trying the untested treatment, but Dr. Galion was brilliant and was making headway with his formulations. Still, communing with the good doctor and allowing him to use his spiritual gifts were two different things.

They reached the dying woman and Dr. Galion spoke for a few minutes about the treatment, its limitations and expectations. He promised nothing but did instill some hope into her. He poured a glass of water and added a small amount of his tincture to it. Even Hydogall didn't know exactly what was in it since many of the doctor's bottles were not clearly marked, but he knew it was based around silver, long known in the ancient world for its limited medicinal properties.

The dying woman sipped it slowly. It obviously burned going down her throat, but she kept drinking. When it was gone, she sat back and smiled. She coughed slightly every now and then, but her demeanor was more content. She said she felt better.

Dr. Galion stayed in the room for the rest of the night. Thad needed to return home since he had business the next morning. Dr. Galion monitored her fever and other vital signs throughout the night, sleeping intermittently in the chair provided by the infirmary staff. He gave her several more tinctures in that time. By morning, the dying woman was feeling somewhat better, though her symptoms had only slightly improved.

The day staff arrived and Dr. Galion gave them instructions to continue monitoring her. He also gave them some of his tincture and instructions on how to administer it every four hours. He would be back later that afternoon.

As he walked back to his laboratory, Dr. Galion smiled proudly. Hydogall noticed the doctor almost skipped along, such was his excited state. When he walked in, he immediately went to his polished serving tray to speak with Hydogall.

"What do you think, Old Boy?" Dr. Galion asked.

"I must admit, I was worried about subjecting her to treatment that was untested, but she seemed to be responding favorably," Hydogall replied. "You may have truly done it this time, Doctor."

Dr. Galion smiled large. "Maybe I have, at that." He stared out the window, seemingly looking into the future. Then he turned to the tray. "I mean, 'we' may have done it. Your help has been immeasurable, Old Boy."

"Thank you, Doctor, but I only suggested you use silver. The formulation is all yours."

Dr. Galion smiled broadly again and relaxed in his padded chair. He soon drifted off to sleep.

Several hours later he awoke to the smell of smoke. Smoke was common enough but the smell of a burning building was well known to all who lived in the city. Dr. Galion ran to the window and peered out only to see a large building engulfed in flames. It was the workhouse. He knew from the size of the flames it would not be extinguished easily if at all. He sat down in his chair hard, putting his head in his hands near the serving tray.

"Those poor people," he murmured quietly.

"I am sure the fire brigade is doing what it can, Doctor." Hydogall said.

"Yes, yes, I know. Many will get out on the fire escapes, but their infirmary was filled last night, including our patient. The staff may panic and many infirmed will perish. Unfortunately, I've seen it before."

"Is there anything we can do?"

"I am not a member of the fire brigade, Hydogall! Besides, the police will not allow anyone in. Even relatives trying to get to the infirmed will likely be turned away. They are lost, I'm afraid." With that, Dr. Galion sat in his easy chair, his head in his hands.

Hydogall thought for a moment. He knew that with his spiritual gifts, Dr. Galion could indeed help. But was it worth it? The power he could release to him had corrupted many good people over the years. Dr. Galion was a good man, but even good men have their limits. However, many lives were in jeopardy, and many more could be saved if the doctors' treatment worked. If the woman died, they would never know. It could set the project back by months which would mean many more lives would be forfeit. He made his decision.

Dr. Galion sat up after a few minutes and looked at the silver tray. "Doctor," Hydogall assured. "I think we can help." He quickly explained the concept of spiritual gifts which ones he could bestow, including the gift all of The Fallen received: Invulnerability to the hottest of fires. This was not considered a gift so much as a curse. The Fallen needed it to survive the fires of Hell. Having it was like a scarlet letter to many of them.

After a few minutes of instruction, Dr. Galion grabbed the tray and tucked it under his shirt. "I'll need your guidance, Old Boy! I only pray that we are not too late!" The doctor ran down the stairway, holding the tray close to him so it didn't fall.

"You do not need to do anything to be invulnerable to fire. That is easy. But you need to concentrate in order to become invisible."

As the doctor ran down the sidewalk, he concentrated on being invisible, just as Hydogall had instructed in his impromptu lesson. Suddenly, his body disappeared from sight. He could still see the dirt swirl under his footfalls, but his feet were not visible. He stumbled for a moment, but caught himself.

"That is good, Doctor! Just remember, if ash collects on you, you will be visible."

"I understand," Dr. Galion replied as he picked up speed. He reached the workhouse and could see exactly what he feared. All of the able-bodied people were streaming down the fire escapes as the top floors were engulfed. The fire brigade was doing its best to get water into the affected floors, and the Bobbies kept anyone from entering the bottom floors, even though they were not on fire yet.

"I can feel the heat from the flames, but they do not hurt," Dr. Galion marveled, obvious wonderment in his voice as he approached the building. He walked right past the Bobbies, then began to run as he got inside. He ran up the stairs, stumbling at first while ascending without being able to see where his footfalls landed. A few stories up he encountered medical workers coming down the stairway.

"Where are your patients?" Dr. Galion yelled at them, forgetting they could not see him.

"Doctor, they hear you but cannot see you."

"Cowards!" he yelled, continuing up the stairs to the third floor. The patients that could walk had gotten out, but a handful of bedridden remained.

"It appears some managed to get out," Hydogall said.

"Yes, but they should have moved them all out. The flames are not even to this part of the building yet.

"They were scared, Doctor."

"So am I, but ..." his voice trailed off.

He ran to his patient and found her still breathing. He easily picked her up and found the jar containing his formulation on the nightstand next to her. He placed it in his pocket and began making his way to the stairway. "We'll come back for the others," he said to Hydogall.

He carried the woman down all three flights quickly, marveling at his somewhat enhanced strength and speed. He gracefully took three and four steps at a time until he was on the ground floor. He ran outside the door, quickly putting the woman into the arms of a Bobbie standing nearby.

"Make yourself useful, man," Dr. Galion instructed thrusting the woman into his arms. The policeman was caught off guard as the woman appeared to float into his grasp. Dr. Galion ran upstairs again and again, bringing the infirmed back down and into someone's unsuspecting arms.

On his final trip, he stood and looked around the floor. All of the patients had been moved. "I guess we are finished, Ol' Boy," he coughed, short of breath.

"There may be others trapped above, Doctor. Shall we take a moment to do a quick perusal?"

"Yes, yes, let's do."

Dr. Galion ascended the stairs, stopping at each level to scan the floors and cry out for occupants. He encountered a lot of burning wood, but was not scorched in the slightest. Finally, he reached the top floor.

He scanned the area which was completely engulfed in flames. He found it harder to breathe.

"Have a care, Doctor. Though the flames cannot hurt you, there is very little free oxygen in the air and lots of ash. You still need to breathe. I suggest crouching a little."

Dr. Galion crouched lower to the floor. He ripped off his shirt sleeve and wrapped it around his mouth and nose. He moved slowly, yelling for any occupants. He heard a faint cough coming from somewhere and searched the open floor until he saw a young girl sitting in the corner, weakly coughing.

Dr. Galion moved to her, picking her up in his arms. She wiggled and screamed slightly, not seeing him. He whispered to her, "Don't worry, child. You have found favor this night. Hug close to me and keep your eyes closed." She did as he instructed.

"Good call, Doctor," Hydogall said, "but I believe our egress to the stairway has been blocked by the flames."

"They will not harm me," he replied.

"No, Doctor, but they will surely harm the girl."

"Drat!" he replied. "The fire escape then!"

He moved quickly to the open windows, finding the landing for the fire escape. He was careful to keep the girl close so she would not be blistered by the white-hot iron railings. He descended as quickly as he could. At the third-floor landing, he stepped inside.

"I can travel faster with her down the regular stairs," he explained. Just then, an explosion rocked the building sending a fireball down the hallway at them. Dr. Galion turned his back to the hot blast as it connected with him, and blew him hard out through the window.

Those gathered below turned their faces from the massive fireball as it exploded out of the side of the building. When they turned back, they saw a figure floating three stories above them. It appeared to be a young girl in a fetal position and she just hovered there. Then she floated down to the ground, coughing as she lay sprawled out on the road.

Hydogall had taken control of Dr. Galion's body in order to help him fly and land. He was still invisible but only got a block or so before he let go of his control, and the doctor's body slid down against a wall and he reappeared. No one noticed with all the confusion.

A few minutes later some of the medical personnel from the infirmary saw his body and ran to assist him. Finding him breathing, they took him to another workhouse infirmary nearby where the wounded were being treated. They assumed he had been in the burning building and had just managed to get out before collapsing from smoke inhalation.

He slept the entire day before waking in his hospital bed that night. The night nurse was sitting nearby and explained what had happened. He was slightly out of sorts, but felt fine. The last thing he remembered was the fireball hitting him in the back.

He felt for the silver serving tray and found nothing. He was wearing a sleeping gown. He asked for his clothes and the night nurse found them in a cloth bag under his chair. No silver tray there either. Being silver, and very expensive, it was likely stolen. Maybe he lost it in the explosion. Maybe it was taken from him as he slept. The jar containing his formulation was there, though.

Despite the nurse's protestations, he rose and dressed. He assured her he felt fine, but agreed to wait for the night physicians' assessment. She left and returned with him, and after a short exam he agreed Dr. Galion would be okay to leave if he felt up to it. He removed the jar from his pocket and explained to the nursing staff how to administer it to his patient, pointing her out among the suffering. He thanked all that were there and left the building.

Dr. Galion was still a little confused and wanted desperately to speak with Hydogall. He knew he could speak with him even with the smallest of silver touching his skin, but he had none. Not even silver jewelry.

Though the doctor was rather well off, thanks to his family's social standing, he had chosen to live in the relatively poor area of the workhouses because it was close to so many sick people, and because the flat had room for a laboratory. His philanthropy in the area gave him good graces in the eyes of many of the inhabitants, but he and his friend Thaddeus Cray still carried pistols when they went out at night. As two men approached from up the sidewalk, Dr. Galion instinctively felt for the revolver and did not find it. It was at home, hidden near his front door.

The taller of the two men tipped his wide-brimmed fedora as he stepped in front of the doctor. "Good evening sir, any small change for the poor?" he asked in a thick cockney dialect.

"I'm sorry," Dr. Galion said. "I have just left the infirmary. I have no money or anything of value on my person."

"That's not the sort of reply we was hopin' for, guvnah," the shorter man grunted. In one quick movement, he grabbed a large knife from his hip and pressed it against the doctor's side. "Surely, you have sumptin' to share, considrin' those fine clothes you are sportin'. Maybe you juss don't wanna share with the likes uh us, huh?"

Dr. Galion was scared but his fear quickly turned to anger. He spent his life helping people. His every day consisted of hard work and determination to help his fellow man. If he wasn't working in his lab, he was volunteering at the infirmaries. Yet these brigands believed he owed them even more? How dare they!

The doctor quickly grabbed the man's hand containing the knife and squeezed hard enough to break both of them.

He let out a howl of pain as the other man moved towards the doctor, a large lead pipe raised. He brought it down and nothing happened. The doctor was no longer there. He was nowhere to be seen. The pipe was removed from the man's hand and it smacked him hard against his head. Once, twice, three times until the man fell to the ground in a heap.

The man with the broken knife and hand was too busy yelling to see what had happened. He felt the pipe hit him and he was out like a light.

The doctor pounded on him several more times on the ground. Then he noticed that on the man's broken and disfigured hand was a large silver ring. He took it off his hand, nearly severing the finger as he did so. He put it on and it disappeared.

"Hydogall, old boy! Are you there?!" he screamed. But there was no reply. He left the two men bleeding profusely on the sidewalk as he walked, invisibly, back to his flat. Luckily, there was no one else on the sidewalk or he may have walked into them. He was listening closely for any words from Hydogall.

He entered his flat and sat in his easy chair. He cranked his phonograph and it began to play a Chopin waltz. He spent several hours trying to summon his friend before he finally drifted off to sleep. He dreamt of the events of that day, his dreams embellishing his deeds somewhat. He got a good, deep sleep that night. The best he had had in ages.

The next morning, he awoke refreshed. He tried talking with Hydogall and there was still no answer. He decided to walk down to get breakfast at a small diner down the street. As he sauntered along, still somewhat listening for Hydogall, he noticed the police looking over the area where he had been attacked. The two men were long gone, but the ground was still covered in blood. He walked up to a Bobbie.

"Excuse me, Sir, what's this all about?" Dr. Galion asked.

Realizing that he was being spoken to by a man of means, the Bobbie answered, "Ghastly business, I'm 'fraid. Two blokes got waylaid last night. Beaten to a bloody pulp. Some workin' girls found them early this morning and called for us."

"Beaten to a pulp, you say? They died, then?"

"'Fraid so. I wouldn't worry too much, though, this kinda thing doesn't happen 'round 'ere too often. Prolly just some vagabonds passing through." The officer looked around the street. "Course, no one saw a thing," he snorted wryly.

"Thank you, Officer," Dr. Galion said as he turned and continued walking. He thought about the scuffle and though he had never been much of a fighter, he hadn't believed he had hit the men with sufficient force to kill them. He supposed it was his enhanced strength that had done it.

Taking a seat outside the small café, he ordered a pastry and some breakfast tea. As he sipped, he continued ruminating on the events of the past two days. He needed to pay a visit to his patient this morning. He had only made a small amount of his formulation, so he needed to make another batch if it looked like his patient was improving. He should also see if the medical staff needs his help with the other patients. It was the proper thing to do after an event such as this.

Suddenly came the realization that he had killed two men. He knew they were dead by his hand, but he hadn't really thought about the moral ramifications. He was a killer! Death was no stranger to him, being a physician, but his entire life was devoted to saving lives, not taking them. Still, they had attacked him and he had only reacted, albeit with much more force than they could have. He supposed he could have just turned invisible and walked away. Certainly, the world was better off without these two ruffians in it. He wondered why he didn't feel something in regard to their deaths. They were human beings after all.

"Well, haven't you got a serious look on your face," came a voice to his rear. Dr. Galion turned to see his friend Thaddeus Cray standing there smiling at him.

"Thaddeus, old man! How are you? Sit, sit," he instructed, motioning to the chair across from him.

"I was actually on my way to check in on you. I was visiting with a client in West End all day and didn't return until late last night. My housekeeper told me about the fire and I wanted to make sure you were alright."

"Oh, I'm perfectly fine. I did try to help out a bit. I managed to get my patient out but was a tad overwhelmed by the smoke. No problem, though, they let me sleep it off in the infirmary before I went home last night. I was just on my way to check on things."

"Well, I'll have a spot of tea with you and accompany you on your rounds, if you don't mind," Thaddeus said jovially.

"Absolutely! I would love the company." It was a lie. Though he did thoroughly enjoy his friends company, he wanted to continue trying to contact Hydogall. Thaddeus didn't know about him, and Dr. Galion didn't want to reveal anything if he didn't have to.

"Say, is that new?" Thaddeus asked, pointing at Dr. Galion's recently acquired silver ring.

Dr. Galion paused before stammering, "Yes…no…not really. It was my father's ring. A silly little thing, but I came across it the other night and it reminded me of him. I put it on this morning for comfort." He didn't like lying to his friend.

Another twenty minutes passed as the two chatted, sipped their tea and ate their pastries. Dr. Galion was hesitant to speak of the previous day's events as he didn't want to accidentally give away too much information. Thaddeus spoke of his visit with his client, a wealthy relative of the royal family. When they finished their food, they walked to the workhouse infirmary located one block over from the one that had burned.

Dr. Galion exchanged pleasantries with the staff, repeatedly thanking them for their good work. He found his patient and, sadly, she had taken a turn for the worse. Either the fire and smoke exacerbated her condition or the formulation simply wasn't working as well as the doctor had hoped. She would likely expire by the end of the day. He spoke with a nurse, reminding her to continue treating her and monitoring her condition. He would be back that evening.

Thaddeus and Dr. Galion spoke about the state of the infirmary and its inhabitants. The doctor told Thaddeus there was nothing more they could do. The patient would likely not make it. Thaddeus was down trodden but managed to keep a stiff upper lip. He told the doctor there was always hope. The two left, walking back to the doctor's flat. They shared a spot of tea and Thaddeus had to leave to meet with a client for lunch.

Dr. Galion spent the rest of the afternoon trying to contact Hydogall and practicing his new abilities. He left briefly to buy a new silver tray and returned home to sit in front of it. It was to no avail. Nothing he did would elicit a reply.

As the night came, he remembered he needed to visit his patient. He grabbed his coat and headed down the stairs and out the door. He briefly thought about taking his revolver, but thought twice. He didn't really need it, after all.

Night had fallen and the streets were dark. There was plenty of activity still. The doctor's walk to the infirmary was uneventful. He reached the infirmary and, as he feared, his patient had died. In his bones knew it wasn't the smoke or the trauma of moving her. The formulation had failed. He arranged for the body to be properly buried and left.

He walked down the sidewalk in deep thought. He looked up when he heard a slight cry from the opposite side of the street. An angry man had slapped a woman and was preparing to do so again. The doctor faded from view as he headed across the narrow street.

Normally something like this in this part of town might elicit from him a 'you there!' or 'hey now!' from across the street. This time, however, the doctor was already angry from his loss. *This poor excuse for an Englishman caught me at a bad time,* he thought.

The man's arm reared back for his next strike. Suddenly, the arm bent back at an unnatural angle against his back. The sound of popping bone and cartilage reverberated down the street, along with the man's bellow. He suddenly fell to the side as his right knee bent inwards from the side, snapping half the ligaments holding it in place. He slumped to the side walk, broken and sobbing. The woman who the man had struck stood in horror. She was joined by several onlookers with mouths agape, staring at the shuddering heap on the ground.

Dr. Galion, pleased at his 'work,' walked away with a spring in his step. The crowd that formed was completely oblivious to him in his current state. He felt alive, like he hadn't in years. He had spent a great deal of his adult life in the laboratory, alone, working tirelessly on a treatment for infections. He had had some successes, but no overreaching treatment that would work for all patients.

It occurred to him that with his new abilities, he had saved more lives in the fire than he had his entire medical career. *Maybe it wasn't my destiny to be a great savior medically but physically instead,* he thought. If only he could speak to Hydogall!

As if on cue, Hydogall voice slowly built in his ears.

"Doctor, can you hear me?"

"Yes, Old Boy, I can!"

"Please, lower you voice to a whisper. We are invisible to their eyes but not their ears."

"Yes, of course," the doctor hurriedly affirmed. "I'll return to my flat so we can speak unabashed." With that, the doctor began to run down the sidewalk until he got to his building. As he entered the door, he remembered to make himself visible again. He went up the stairs and into his flat, running to the serving tray still sitting by his easy chair, where he plopped down.

"There we are, Old Boy," he said, looking at his reflection in tray. "Now tell me, why couldn't I reach you? I was worried."

The image he saw was his own, but it looked tired and gaunt. "I am sorry, Doctor. We never spoke about what would happen if I took over your body without consent. The blast threw us out of the window, knocking you unconscious. I was able to take control to ensure you two landed safely and were not seen. Unfortunately, doing so uses a great deal of energy, and the result leaves me immobilized, dormant, for a time. The longer I have control, the longer I lay dormant. I can still experience everything, but I cannot communicate. It is not unlike paralysis."

"Well, thank you for doing so. You saved both our necks. The girl is doing well at the infirmary."

"I know, Doctor. I see what you see."

"Oh, yes, very good," the doctor stammered.

"Doctor, I am worried about your reaction to my spiritual gifts. Your attack on the man who struck the young lady was particularly vicious. It was unlike you."

The doctor thought for a moment. "Yes, I did let out my inner savage, didn't I? But he won't be putting hands on another woman again, will he?" the doctor joked.

"You are a physician, Sir! You likely crippled that man."

"He'll walk again, but never the same way. He'll have a constant reminder to be a proper gentleman, won't he? So, will the other sots that saw what happened. No one will know how it happened, but they'll know why. Maybe this neighborhood will be just a bit safer for women now."

"Perhaps you are right, Doctor," Hydogall conceded. He was worried, though. The reason he rarely activated his spiritual gifts was for this very reason. Power had the ability to change good men for the worse. He had purposely hidden his ability to fly from the doctor. He might tell him at a later date, but for now, he was going to watch and see how Dr. Galion handled his new abilities.

The two continued talking for a while, both happy to have the chance. Though they had only been speaking for a few months, they had been each other's constant companions. They spoke as old friends.

Hydogall had only been inhabiting the doctor for a year. Dr. Galion had been visiting an infirmary where Hydogall's current Vessel was passing on. He had indwelled him for nearly sixty years and, as was his usual custom, had never revealed himself. When Dr. Galion had passed by his bed, he recognized his status as a Vessel and moved into him.

Eventually the doctor grew tired and went to bed. He lay there for a few minutes before drifting off. His dreams, however, were fitful. He was inundated with images of people being beaten and robbed, raped and murdered on the streets outside. He awoke just a few hours after he had gone to bed.

He arose and dressed. He wore no topcoat nor a hat. He walked towards the door, leaving the revolver in its hidden space. As he walked down the stairs, he faded from view. His determined look would have been the last thing anyone saw before he was completely invisible.

It was Hydogall's custom to always be spoken to first. He considered it a sign of respect to his Vessel, a way for them to feel some sense of privacy. He observed what the doctor was doing, but did not comment.

The doctor walked unnoticed down the sidewalk, and into the dark alleyways no one entered at this time of night unless they were up to no good. As he crisscrossed the many connected alleyways, he found some people sleeping, some drinking heavily and others engaged in other, more physical activities. They sickened the doctor, but, alas, did not seem to be in any distress, so he ignored them.

He turned a corner and found two men beating another rather savagely. He didn't know the reason, but two men against another was hardly fair. He smiled slightly and quickly returned their savagery and then some. Their battered bodies lay on the ground as he departed.

A few blocks over he intervened in an argument between two drunk men. They both had long knives pulled, and he simply knocked their heads together rendering them unconscious. Hydogall took notice that the doctor didn't bother to check their limp bodies for signs of life.

Further up the block, a prostitute was discussing her fee with a potential customer. The doctor kicked the man in his groin with enough force to lift man off the ground nearly a foot. He collapsed in pain. The doctor chuckled quietly. This time Hydogall took note of how long the doctor stared at the prostitute before departing.

By the time the doctor returned to his flat, he had interceded in more than a dozen muggings, assaults, and other unsavory acts. It was a night of blood and broken bones. The doctor was elated, smiling big as he dressed for his slumber. He scrubbed the blood from his knuckles and scraped the flesh from under his nails. He settled into his warm bed, content in knowing that he had made a positive difference in his community.

Hydogall was conflicted. The doctor had undoubtedly saved lives tonight. However, the savagery and excitement he displayed during his attacks worried him. Still, he believed the doctor was a good man at heart. Hopefully, as he adjusted to his new reality, he would again focus on his laboratory work and less on his 'policing.'

Unfortunately, the doctors 'night excursions' continued over the next week. He slept most of the days, rising only to eat and relieve himself. As night would fall he would wake and ready himself. He would spend many hours walking the streets and alleys, and had even traveled by taxi to neighborhoods far worse than his own. On top of the violence, the doctor had taken to stealing a kiss or caress from women he had just saved, believing it was 'owed' to him for his 'chivalrous act.' He and Hydogall had argued that point on more than one occasion.

***

Thaddeus Cray stopped by the doctors flat during one of those late afternoon arguments. He had tried to visit his friend another time, but the sleeping doctor didn't answer the door. As he neared the door, he heard the sound of two voices engaged in sharp discourse. When he knocked, the doctor answered and upon entry found only the doctor inside. When questioned, the doctor laughed and replied that he was working on a new formulation and was working out the details with himself aloud.

Thaddeus convinced his friend to go out for a quick bite and catch up. They hadn't seen each other over the past week. Thaddeus was interested in the doctor's new formulation, while the doctor, whose demeanor was less cerebral and more brutish than normal, only wanted to talk about how much safer the streets were. As they ate their food, the doctor continued speaking.

"Just look at the passersby, Old Boy. Everyone seems happier lately."

84

"Indeed. I've noticed that, too. Must be this vigilante business everyone's on about."

"Vigilante, you say? I haven't heard anything about that."

"Oh yes, apparently someone is stalking around during the night, beating people senseless if they are breaking the law. A few of the victims have died."

"Died? That's terrible." The doctor feigned horror but, in reality, couldn't have cared less about them. Those men that died had been particularly heinous vagabonds.

"Not really, they were very bad men. People are happy about it for the most part."

"For the most part? Are there dissenters?"

"There always are, to be sure. I guess some people worry that no one has ever seen the vigilante. He hides in the shadows very well, moves too fast to be seen. People fear what they don't know." Thaddeus pursed his lips and looked down. "Some of the women have charged he inappropriately touched them after saving their necks. Some say he groped them or stole a kiss. Who can say, really? They were pretty scared. Some were very inebriated."

"I'll just bet," the doctor replied, a wry smile beginning to form on his face.

Thaddeus noticed the smile, but thought nothing more of it. "The police don't know what to think. Since he hasn't actually been seen, I don't think they believe he exists. Or they're just happy for the help." Thaddeus noticed the doctor's eyes wandering around the café and lingering on many of the women.

"Is everything alright, doctor?"

"Why do you ask?" the doctor replied without taking his eyes off the buxom waitress across the room.

"You just seem…out of sorts."

The doctor continued to stare at the women for a few more seconds and then, as if waking from a dream, suddenly blinked a few times, stiffened up and looked over at Thaddeus. "Sorry, Old Boy. I guess I've been cooped up in the lab to much lately. Not as good a view up there as there is in here, right?" He slapped Thaddeus on the arm and chuckled.

"Yes," Thaddeus acquiesced warily, "quite right." He was beginning to worry about his friend. It was unlike him to make such vulgar comments. Even the way he sat in his chair, slouching with his legs spread wide and lap exposed, was so very different from the norm. He usually sat up straight and looked you in the eye as you spoke. He looked as if he hadn't even shaved in a week.

"Tell me, Doctor, how is your research going? Do you have a new formulation yet?"

"I'm afraid not," Dr. Galion replied. "To tell you the truth, I'm a little discouraged after what happened to my last patient. It's almost like God himself doesn't want me to succeed."

"Oh, don't say that, Doctor. Yours is a righteous endeavor. Certainly the Almighty, above all others, can see that. In fact, He may have aided you already in ways we cannot fathom." Thaddeus was a faithful man to the core. And he really felt this way about the doctor.

"Fat lotta good it's done me so far," the doctor said. This was the final straw for Thaddeus. The doctor was not one to blaspheme. Something was very wrong with his friend.

"Are you sure you alright, Old Boy?"

"Perfectly," the doctor replied incredulously.

"It's just that, you seem different somehow. Almost angry in a way. You are not feeling out of sorts?"

The doctor laughed out loud. "I can honestly say I feel better than I ever have. More focused! More driven!"

"I'm glad to hear it," Thaddeus replied. "The world needs you and your research." Thaddeus let it go, but he was still concerned. His friend's demeanor had changed completely, almost as if he were a different person.

The two finished their supper and walked back towards the doctor's flat. It was dark outside and while Thaddeus studied his surroundings as they walked, Dr. Galion seemed completely comfortable and oblivious to any danger that might be lurking in the shadows. He was loud and boisterous, like a drunkard, though he had had no spirits with his dinner.

Soon, they were at the doctors building and the two parted. Thaddeus worried about his friend and as he crossed the street looked back at him once more. Curiously, he saw the doctor had not walked into his flat, but had moved down the sidewalk instead. He decided to follow and see where he was going. Neither of them liked to be out at night in this neighborhood. Luckily, Thaddeus had his revolver tucked under his coat.

The doctor only walked a few blocks before ducking into an alley. Thaddeus followed and peeked around the corner. Though dark, he could see to the end of the alley and it appeared completely empty! Thaddeus was dumbfounded. There was no way, even running at full speed that the doctor could have gotten down the alley and out of sight that quickly without being seen.

Thaddeus reluctantly stepped into the alley and walked to the end. It broke off into two different directions. One side was very short, opening at a busy street. The other direction was longer and even darker. He went down the darker path, filled with concern for his friend.

This alley was not empty. There were people here and there, obviously under the influence of alcohol or opium. Ladies halfheartedly propositioned him as he walked by and he ignored them. His hand subconsciously moved towards the revolver.

Thaddeus was suddenly struck with the realization that his friend was likely taking opium. He had some experience with these types of people, volunteering to represent them in court as a young lawyer. The doctor's sudden change in demeanor was easily attributed to the use of the illicit drug. He had to help him!

He moved further down the alley, his eyes constantly shifting from side to side. Further up the way, he heard a woman scream. Though he was scared, he moved forward more quickly. There was little light now, but he could just see the outline of some people shuffling about up ahead. As he neared the scene, he saw a man on the ground bleeding profusely. There was also a woman, her back against the wall of a building. She was still screaming as she looked around. She suddenly jerked to the left and fell on her back. She acted as if she was being pushed down, but there was no one there.

Thaddeus cried out, "What the devil is going on!?"

Some cursing could be heard, again seemingly from nowhere. The woman rocked to her side and gasped as if a weight had been lifted. Thaddeus saw a splash in the puddle in front of him and he was struck hard across the nose. He fell backwards to into a wall. He was stunned, but was able to grab his revolver. Through tears he squinted to see anything as a second blow hit him in the forehead. He closed his eyes and fired three shots directly in front of him. He heard footfalls running away as he blacked out.

When Thaddeus awoke, it was very dark still. The girl that had been attacked was stooping next to him, holding his hand. People were moving all around, including the police. The girl saw his stirring and informed the officer standing nearby.

"How do you feel, Sir?" he asked.

"My head stings a little, but otherwise I am fine," Thaddeus said, running his hands around his upper body.

"Thank God for that," the policeman marveled. "Looks like you spoiled an assault of some sort, but we are still sortin' it all out. The lass says she was walkin' home from work when a man grabbed her. Says she screamed and he pulled back to strike her. According to the girl, his head suddenly twisted hard. Was that your doin'?"

"When I arrived, the man was on the ground already. So was the girl." Thaddeus rubbed his head.

"She said as much, but I thought she may a' been hysterical. She says his neck just broke, like someone twisted it, but there weren't no one there. I assumed she just didn't see you."

"No, sir, she is spot on." Thaddeus rubbed his head some more.

"Then you were responsible for the shooting?"

"Yes, I was able to get off three shots, I believe." Thaddeus felt his coat for his revolver and didn't find it.

"Here is your revolver, Sir. I checked it and there are three spent casings." He handed the revolver to Thaddeus. "Tell me, Sir, what were you shootin' at exactly?"

"I'm sure I don't know. It was as if someone were there, but I couldn't see him. The puddles were splashing, there was talking and I was hit. I shot blindly, I'm sorry to say."

"Well, I dug two slugs out o' the wall and I think the other may have hit home. There is a blood trail that starts down the alley. We followed it but it ended before the street, I'm sad to say."

The officer made some notes in his pad and asked Thaddeus a few more questions. After an hour, Thaddeus was told he could leave. As he walked out of the alley, he remembered why he had been in there in the first place. He ran towards Dr. Galion's' laboratory.

As he neared the door, he saw blood. He withdrew his revolver and walked slowly up the stairs. The door was open at the top and he crept in. The shades were open, providing plenty of early morning light to the interior. Sitting in a chair by the window was the doctor.

"Thaddeus," Dr. Galion said. "I'm so glad you are okay."

Thaddeus raised his revolver. "What is going on, Doctor? That was you in the alley, wasn't it?"

"Yes, yes, Old Boy. And now I will receive my just desserts." The doctor told his friend everything. He demonstrated his ability to become invisible. He let Hydogall speak. Everything was laid bare before his friend.

Thaddeus was in awe. He wondered how this could have been happening under his nose. He slumped down in a chair directly across from the doctor, all but forgetting the revolver in his hand. Then he remembered the blood. "Paul, we have to get you to the infirmary!"

"No, my friend, it is too late. Your shot hit its mark. I have a large hole in my belly and I'll be dead soon. Nothing my fellow physicians could do now but give me a dose of morphine for the pain."

Thaddeus was not surprised. The amount of blood beneath the chair was substantial. "Still, the pain must be intense." He had tears in his eyes as he spoke.

"No more than I deserve, I'm afraid. I must admit, I am scared to meet my Maker. My whole life I have tried to do good, but just the smallest taste of power and I was completely corrupted. Hydogall, will my final judgment be harsh?"

"Your 'Maker' looks at everything you have done in your life. The Father is nothing if not fair. But He and He alone may judge you."

Dr. Galion asked, "And what of you, my friend? What will become of you when I am gone?"

"Thaddeus is also a Vessel. It's probably one of the reasons why you two were so close. If it is alright with him, I would like to dwell within him."

Dr. Galion saw the shocked look on Thaddeus' face. "It's not so bad, Ol' Boy. In fact, you will hardly know he is there unless he speaks. You will only possess the abilities that corrupted me if he allows it."

"I suppose it would be alright," Thaddeus conceded unsurely. He believed he owed it to the doctor, since he was responsible for his life ending.

They sat together by the window speaking and praying together for nearly a half hour before the doctor drifted off. After a few minutes, Thaddeus checked for a pulse and found none. He removed the silver ring from his friend and placed it on his own finger.

"Are you there, Hydogall?" he asked into the air.

"Yes, Thaddeus. I am here whenever you need me."

"That is an odd sensation, talking to oneself and receiving an answer."

"If it helps, you can just pretend I am not here," Hydogall offered.

"No, at least for now, I would like the company. Tell me, my new friend, do you like Chopin?"

Chapter 6 – Onward and Upward

"Did anyone ever find out about the doctor? What he had done?" Dylan asked.

"No, Thaddeus had a friend who was a policeman, and he called him to do the investigation," Hydogall replied. "Thaddeus told them the doctor was still alive when he had arrived, and recounted a story of a burglar shooting him. No one questioned it. Not even the policeman whom he had interacted with earlier. The doctor was a good man, sadly corrupted by power."

"And Thaddeus told the story to Robert Louis Stevenson?"

"Yes, he was a client and an author of some repute. One night over drinks, Thaddeus recounted the story, changing the names and events slightly. Mr. Stevenson was enamored by the tale and asked if he could write a story based on it. Thaddeus agreed."

"And what about me? Will I be corrupted so easily?"

"I do not believe so. Remember, I had not known the doctor very long, but I have been with you most of your life. I may not hear your thoughts, but I have observed you and your deeds. Like Thaddeus Cray, you are truly a fine man."

"Thanks," Dylan said. They sat in silence for a few minutes then Dylan was asleep.

The next morning Dylan awoke, and began his normal routine. The only real deviation he made was when he showered he kept his eyes on the ceiling. He knew it was silly, but he felt compelled to do it anyway, at least at first. He didn't speak to Hydogall until he was walking to the door.

He spoke in a low tone. "Good morning, Hydogall." It was almost a question.

"Good Morning, Dylan." The voice was the same measured cadence it had been the night before. "No need for the hushed tones. I do not sleep. I am always here."

Dylan thought about that for a second. He supposed it was like having a guardian angel, no pun intended. *At least my thoughts are my own,* he thought.

He grabbed his jacket and messenger bag, and walked to his bus stop. The bus arrived on schedule and he nodded to the bus driver, whose name he still couldn't remember. He sat near the back, the bus having only one other passenger who sat up near the driver. Then he had an odd thought.

"Hydogall," he whispered. "Do you remember the bus driver's name?"

"His name is Sam. You asked him the first time you got on, but have never used it," Hydogall whispered back.

"Do you remember everything you hear?"

"I remember everything I have experienced since the moment I was created."

Dylan's eyes got wide. "That is amazing!" he said under his breath.

As they arrived at their stop, Dylan arose and walked toward the front exit. "Thanks for the ride, Sam."

"Anytime, Sir," Sam stated with a wide smile.

Dylan continued on to his building. He entered and immediately saw Neville readying his backpack. He asked, "Anything to report, Corporal?"

Neville pulled off his headphones and snapped to attention, responding, "Perimeter is tight, all floors are secure, Sir!" Dylan returned the salute.

"Roger that," Dylan replied then moved towards the stairs. He walked up the two flights to his office. He said a few 'good mornings' on the way to his office then opened the door. The lights sprang on as usual. He sat his bag down and looked at his watch as he opened the side door to his lab. He waited a full minute before the technology lit up as programmed.

Dylan spent the morning studying data and lecturing. After his morning class had cleared out, he glanced at his phone and noticed a text message from Rusty.

Rusty: Lunch?

Dylan: Sure. Where?

Rusty: My office. I have a pizza.

Dylan: Sounds good. See you in 5.

Dylan walked briskly towards his office to drop off his bag, and then walked to the History Building next door where Rusty had his office. Technically it was the Social Science and Anthropology building, but most people just called it the History Building. Rusty's office was on the ground floor and the door was open.

When he stepped in, he saw that Patty was there. He had purposely not contacted her this morning, giving her some space after everything that had happened the day before. He was glad she was there, and she smiled when he walked in.

Rusty's office was actually two large offices. At his request, the dividing wall had been removed and the interior was filled with large filing cabinets and glass cases containing various relics currently under study. The large, round table in the middle of the room was usually covered with paperwork but had been cleaned off for their lunch. Dylan stepped in and closed the door behind him.

"Dylan, my friend, have a seat before the pizza gets cold!" Rusty instructed, motioning to the open chair next to Patty. She stood and they shared quick hug. He sat and took a large slice of pepperoni pizza out of the box.

"Thanks," he said, "I'm starving."

"Well, you're eating for two," Patty contributed almost mindlessly.

There was a short, awkward pause. Then Dylan snorted and all three began to laugh heartedly. As the laughter died down, Rusty spoke while Dylan and Patty ate.

"In all seriousness, you are going to need some training to deal with Dagnem."

"Sounds like you have a plan, Rusty," Patty inquired.

"I have a cabin outside of town. Very isolated, no prying eyes, no cameras. If we can spend a few days there, I think I can get you ready."

"Just a few days?" Dylan asked.

"Well, it's all we have, my friend. The first body was discovered this morning."

"What?" Patty, Dylan, and Hydogall asked at the same time.

"Yes, I heard about it this morning. A woman, probably homeless. Heart missing. Found along the railroad tracks. It was on the radio.

All were silent for a moment. "I thought we would have more time," Dylan lamented in a low tone.

"I'm afraid not, but we do have something he doesn't know about?"

"You?" Patty asked.

"Well, yes, but I was referring to the fact that Dagnem doesn't know that Dylan and Hydogall have met. He believes Hydogall's Vessel will be easy to kill because he is unaware of what is happening. But we know him and we know what he can do and we can devise our plan of attack based on that. The only thing we don't know is who his Vessel is."

They spent the rest of the afternoon planning their time at the cabin. They could leave tonight since neither taught classes on Friday. They sketched out some ideas on the whiteboard and came up with a brief plan.

By the time they had finished, it was early evening. Patty drove Dylan home, then left to pack some things for the trip. Dylan grabbed a gym bag and packed a few things.

"I would suggest you bring your ski goggles," Hydogall requested.

"Why?" Dylan asked.

"When you are flying, the wind dries your eyes out."

"That's something I never would have thought of."

"That's why I am here," Hydogall said. "Some warm clothes and thick socks are not a bad idea either."

"Good idea. It can get cool this time of year and probably more so up in the air."

Dylan packed his thick socks and ski pants, but decided on a leather jacket instead of the thick ski jacket, since it was too bulky. Some suede gloves rounded out his gear.

A few minutes later, Patty was honking her car horn outside. Dylan locked up and they drove north of town and before long were in the surrounding hills. Rusty had given them detailed instructions on how to reach his cabin and twenty miles outside of town, they turned onto a dirt road they had almost missed. After a half mile, the road turned to asphalt again, and soon they were there. Rusty's old car was parked in front.

The cabin was nicer than Dylan had imagined it would be. The area was relatively flat with hills on all sides and some trees. It felt like you were completely isolated from the world. The cabin itself was two story, and built to look like a typical log cabin. It was probably a couple of decades old but in good shape. It had solar panels and several satellite dishes on top. There was also a large, metal shop building alongside it.

They parked and grabbed their bags. They walked towards the large porch and Rusty came out the door to meet them. As Dylan walked in, he noticed how thick the door was. Rusty showed them around, the interior being decorated as eclectically as his house in town. Rusty took them upstairs to some empty bedrooms and they unpacked. Dylan's room was decorated with an Old West theme. He assumed the décor was probably authentic, and there was probably a story attached to every item.

He sat his bag on the bed and walked to the large window. It was a beautiful view, if you like desolation. Rolling hills with a smattering of trees here and there. He leaned against the window sill and noticed a small handle coming from each side of the pane. He pulled them slightly and saw metal shutters attached. He pulled them together and the window was completely blocked by half-inch thick metal. They clicked into place and locked tight.

Dylan thought about the shutters for a minute. He had never seen this before on a cabin. Sure, some small hunter's cabins had wooden shutters you could nail in place for winter to keep bears out, but these were way beyond that. He hunted around the pane and noticed a foot pedal near the floor. He stepped on it and the shutters snapped back a few inches apart. He grabbed the handles and opened them all the way again.

He examined the pane more thoroughly, and noticed something he hadn't before. The wall was easily more than a foot thick. The logs on the outside were a façade. Apparently, the walls were filled with something other than wood.

He turned to the bed and unpacked. It was getting dark outside, and he walked down to Patty's room. The door was open, but he knocked anyway. She turned and saw him and motioned for him to come inside.

As he approached her, she spoke in hushed tones. "This place is a fortress," she observed, patting the walls.

"I know. Did you see the steel shutters on the windows?" Dylan asked.

"No," she said walking over and finding the same handles. "Weird," she added pulling them out slightly. "The walls are thicker than anything I have ever seen. And did you notice the door when we came in? Or the doors to the bedrooms?"

"Yeah," Dylan replied. "Built to take a beating."

Downstairs, Rusty yelled for them to come down for dinner. They went down and found the table already set and food on the table. The sat and Rusty said Grace.

As they ate, Rusty explained the history of the cabin. "I'm sure you noticed that this cabin is not all it seems to be. I bought it about ten years ago from a Survivalist friend of mine. He was preparing for the end of the world, and ran out of money before he could finish it. I offered to loan him the money to finish it, but he lost interest in the Survivalist lifestyle and offered to sell me the cabin and the land. I had it finished and upgraded, and now it's my home away from home."

"It's beautiful, Rusty." Patty acknowledged.

"It's probably too big for me, but now you are here, too. You two may use it any time you like. We'll enter your fingerprints into the electronic lock after dinner. I want you to be comfortable."

"That's very generous. Thank you," Dylan stated.

They finished their meal and chatted about work a bit. Then Rusty excused himself and returned with a platter of coffee cups and three pieces of pie. "I thought we could eat dessert on the porch."

Dylan moved to take the platter, but Rusty shrugged him off saying, "Oh, it's not heavy. And I'm not as feeble as I look."

Dylan responded, "you don't look feeble, Rusty." Again, Rusty shrugged him off and laughed. They all three moved outside and found chairs.

It was a beautiful evening. The moon had not risen yet and the stars were clear as could be. Dylan pointed out some planets and they even saw some satellites flying over.

Suddenly, Dylan stood up and insisted, "well, I've put it off long enough." He walked off the porch and passed the cars. He looked to the sky and slowly began to rise. He stopped about fifty feet from the ground and looked around.

Rusty and Patty both moved quickly off the porch and peered up at him. As Patty was about to call up to him, he shot up another one hundred feet.

"Dylan, are you crazy!" she shouted. She couldn't see him in the dark sky. "This is not baby steps!"

Suddenly, they could see a bright light high up in the sky. It moved backwards and forwards, zigzagging around the property for nearly ten minutes. It went higher up and out over the hills, then back. Slowly the light came down towards them. Soon, they could see the light was Dylan's cell phone.

"I forgot a flashlight," he declared touching down smoothly.

Patty ran towards him and hugged him tightly. "Are you OK?" she asked.

"Yeah," Dylan confirmed. "It's not like Superman. My whole body is just moving from place to place. It felt like a roller coaster as I moved, lots of inertia. Hydogall was talking me through it, helping me to remember to start slow and end slow. He was right, though, I should have put on the ski goggles and jacket."

"You were doing very well, my friend. It is not an easy task. Our human bodies were not meant for such things, and our brains have a tough time comprehending the input."

"Flying at night is definitely not easy. I almost hit the side of the hills. Moonlight might help. I was thinking it would be easier to conceal my flight at night, but if I have to use a flashlight it kind of defeats the purpose."

"You looked more at ease this time," Patty said.

"I was. Hydogall helped me work through it at home a bit, and tonight I just decided to throw caution to the wind and go for it."

Rusty chortled. "What'd I say?" Dylan asked.

Rusty laughed again. "The phrase 'throw caution to the wind.' It actually comes from *Paradise Lost* by Milton. That poem is about Adam and Eve being thrown out of the garden."

"Lovely," Patty smirked sarcastically.

"No more talk about such things," Rusty said. "Tonight we enjoy each other's company and tomorrow we get to work. Who wants another glass of wine?"

Patty and Dylan exchanged shrugs. They walked up the porch stairs and sat down. The evening was brisk but not cold. They all three gazed out into the darkness, secretly hoping it wasn't gazing back.

***

The man indwelling Dagnem walked around the campus of Bridger Community College. He could tell this was some area of importance for Hydogall. Hydogall! The name left a bad taste in his mind. Was he indwelling a student? A professor maybe? Possibly some other staff?

He walked around the quad area looking at the buildings. He had seen such things come and go in his many years. Still, the brick architecture was nice. When he came to the Physics and Astronomy building, he knew he had found where his prey spent most of his time. The door was locked and a janitor was visible inside. *No need to make a fuss now,* he thought. He could come back during the day just as easily. Besides, the night was young and there were so many choices on the menu.

Chapter 7 – Fine Tuning

Dylan stood on the hill with Patty and Rusty, dressed in his hiking boots, dark brown ski pants, a leather jacket, brown suede gloves, and ski goggles.

"I feel ridiculous," Dylan announced.

"You look hot," Patty replied. Rusty smiled.

"It's not even that cold," Dylan said.

"It's Wyoming, Dylan. That outfit works almost year-round," Patty chuckled, only half joking.

"Dylan, I have been in wars too numerous to count. I've been clothed in metal, leather, khaki, and even wood. Our foe is as strong as you are. The jacket and pants you brought are flexible enough to give you full range of motion but thick enough to deflect most slashing blades. And like Patty said, if you need to blend in, you probably could."

"I can turn invisible. I don't have to blend in," Dylan stated and smiled. "Wow that sounds crazy out loud."

"You are planning for many eventualities. It may not be prudent to be invisible all the time. Hydogall, can you explain it?"

"I think so, Rusty," Hydogall started. "Keep in mind that when I was a Watcher, the world was a smaller place. Many fewer people even in the 'civilized' areas. Our goal was always to blend in. Since we appear human, we had only to don clothing appropriate to the region. Sometimes, we smeared dirt or dung on our robes. If we were in a drinking establishment, we drank. If we were at a temple, we prayed and sacrificed. It helped us to be part of the moment and not just a dispassionate observer. It would have been easy to just stay invisible, but our perspective would not have been the same."

Dylan thought about Hydogall's words for a moment, and relented. "Okay, okay, you're right. I've seen plenty of people dressed like this around town, just not usually so late in the spring. But I reserve the right to revisit this at some point in the future."

"Agreed," Rusty replied. "Now I want you to practice taking off and landing on different surfaces and at different speeds. The house, the hills, the trees, those rocky outcroppings. Then try flying around obstacles. When you feel comfortable with all that, join us in the shop."

As Patty and Rusty walked down the hill and into the shop, Dylan began to do as instructed. He spent nearly an hour going over and over the moves until he felt comfortable. He was doing somersaults in the air and perching atop tall trees. He flew through the tree line, dodging in and out of the trees doing his best Superman imitation, with his body horizontal and both of his arms outstretched in front of him. He couldn't help but have a big smile on his face. He was having a blast, until he flew through a cloud of mosquitos. He had to pause to wipe the splattered remnants off of his face and goggles. Then he flew to the open shop door.

He landed just outside the building. Just as his feet touched ground, he was hit in the middle of the chest by a tennis ball. It stung a little and he looked up to see Rusty pointing a tennis ball launcher at him. He fired another and Dylan moved to the side catching a glancing shot off of his ribs.

"What the heck, Rusty?!" Dylan yelled. Rusty fired volley after volley, striking Dylan again and again until he finally missed. Then he missed again and again and again.

Rusty stopped firing. "Look at your feet," he instructed, pointing. Dylan looked down and realized he was floating. "You are actually faster and more maneuverable in the air than on the ground. You can use that," Rusty said.

"You could have just told me instead of shooting me first."

"I wanted to see if your reflexes would take over. And they did. It may not shoot bullets, but these babies are hard to dodge."

"You looked like you were having fun up there," Patty observed.

"I was, Patty. When you're a kid reading a comic book or watching a movie where people can fly, you imagine how great it would be. It's even more exhilarating than that. In fact…" He suddenly scooped her up in his arms and flew out of the door. They soared high into the air. At first Patty clutched him tightly and buried her face, but began to release a little and peak out as they slowed their ascent.

"Take a look, Patty. Isn't it an incredible view?"

Patty turned her head without letting go of his neck. "It's, it's amazing, Dylan." Her eyes were wide and she got more comfortable when she realized how tightly she was being held.

They began to rotate slowly as they drank in the scenery. At first glance, this part of Wyoming could be off-putting to visitors. Its sparse rolling hills with a smattering of trees here and there made it seem almost lifeless at first glance. Those that made it their home, though, knew the incredible abundance of life that called this area home. With flora and fauna as diverse as it was plentiful, sometimes you had to get above it to really let its splendor sink in. The brochures called it 'Big Sky Country' and it was not hard to see why.

After a few more moments together, they meandered downward and back in front of the shop. Patty gave Dylan a quick peck on the cheek as they walked inside, hand in hand.

"Thank you for flying Mathis Air," he chuckled.

She giggled as she walked towards the small kitchenette. "I'm going to make some iced tea. Sound good to you fellas?

"Sure," they both replied in unison.

Rusty was smiling as he approached Dylan. "So, Dylan, you are a scientist, what did you learn from your practice?"

"Like Hydogall and you were saying, the more you do it, the easier it is. One drawback though is that it is hard to hear Hydogall while flying. The wind noise is terrible."

Rusty rubbed his chin. "Maybe a full helmet would be better. Like a motorcycle helmet. Less wind noise and your voices would be contained. I've seen some that have two way radios built into them so riders can communicate with each other," Rusty said. "We could talk to you, too, when you are flying."

"That would probably work, but I would look foolish carrying a motorcycle helmet around with me. I don't even own a motorcycle."

Rusty looked around the shop. "How about that one?"

Dylan looked to where Rusty was pointing. There was something sitting in the corner covered by a dusty tarp. Rusty walked over to it and Dylan followed. Rusty pulled on the tarp and exposed an old motorcycle with a side car.

"This is a 1941 BMW R75. It was used by the Germans during World War 2. I was part of an infantry battalion that helped liberate several concentration camps. My best friend and I 'liberated' a motorcycle just like that from some German guards and we used it to ferry messages back and forth. They are nearly indestructible and *so* fast. About thirty years ago, I bought this one and had it restored. I even put our names on the sidecar like pilots do to their fighter jets."

Dylan bent down and read the names. "Private Hodges. Private Larabie." Dylan looked questionably at Rusty.

"I was Private Larabie. Private Russell Larabie. The long-lived, often have to change their names. My friend was Hodges. Private Hiram Hodges. We used to joke that he must have had a

Jewish ancestor with a name like Hiram. He was a great friend and an incredible soldier. He actually fell in love with a gypsy girl the Nazi's had trussed up in one of the camps. They did unspeakable things to those women, experimented on them in the most horrendous of ways. When I saw how in love they were, I offered to help sneak her out of Europe and into the United States. I had some friends that had been sneaking Jews out of Eastern Europe earlier in war. Of course, it was a lot easier back then. They got her out and they reunited later. Lived the rest of their lives in a small town in California."

"I imagine you have a lot of stories like that, Rusty." Dylan turned to the motorcycle. "But I can't take this bike. It's just too nice. Don't get me wrong, I love it. I've always wanted a motorcycle. But this one, it would stick out too much. I would be afraid of it getting stolen. I need to find something simpler and cheaper. I'll get the helmet, though, for now. There's a motorcycle dealer in town. I'm sure they have them."

"Well, I'll leave it to you in my Will," Rusty said, laughing.

"I'll take it," Dylan replied, also laughing.

Both men walked over to where Patty had just finished pouring some iced tea. Dylan drank down the whole glass and poured some more.

"I have to run into Laramie for a few hours," Patty explained. "My Master Professor needs my help grading some research papers this afternoon. Nothing like working on a Saturday. Can I pick up anything while I'm there, Rusty?"

"I think I have everything we need."

"I'll walk you to your car," Dylan said. They went inside the house to retrieve her purse and then walked to her car.

"Don't work too hard," Dylan half-joked, giving her a hug.

"You either," she replied. Then she got in and drove away.

Dylan and Rusty had a quick lunch then continued training. Rusty had spread a tarp down in the shop and was showing Dylan some Krav Maga moves. Several times Dylan had the wind knocked out of him. Indeed, Rusty was very spry for someone who looked like he could have started collecting social security ten years ago. They worked for several hours, and soon Dylan had mastered several effective attack and defense moves.

After a short break, Dylan decided he needed more practice being invisible. He was flying at first, but landed in a small stretch of dense forest. He began to jog through the trees, getting used to anticipating where his feet would fall, jumping over fallen logs and dodging low branches. He got a lot of cuts and scrapes, and fell a few times, but he soon got the hang of it.

He stopped to catch his breath and heard a rumble in the distance coming from the cabin. He took to the air and arced up and over the hill towards the sound. He found Rusty sitting on the old motorcycle, wearing an old-style leather pilot cap with goggles.

"What's going on?" Dylan asked.

"I think it's time to see how fast you can fly. This baby can hit one hundred miles per hour on the open road. How about we head over to the highway and you try and keep up with this old man?"

"Sounds good," Dylan agreed.

They rode and flew the half mile or so down the dirt road to the deserted single lane highway. Once Rusty hit the pavement, he gunned the bike north towards a long, straight stretch. At first, Dylan had trouble catching up, but soon he did. It wasn't easy to watch ahead of him keep an eye on Rusty, but he did it.

He couldn't see the speedometer, but he did notice a huge grin on Rusty's' face. He was absolutely enjoying himself. Suddenly, up ahead, a car appeared from around a bend in the road. Dylan instinctively turned invisible. Rusty slowed down as the red and blue lights came on.

Dylan hovered above as the officer spoke with Rusty about his speed. He could hear the exchange very well, but kept moving around above them.

"Dr. Carlson, Sir, we've talked about your speeding out here," the officer said.

"This is Wyoming, Jimmy. One of the few bastions of freedom left in this country. You can't blame an old man for wanting to see if he still had the moxie."

"We both know you have plenty of moxie, Doc, but you really need to be careful. You were approaching a hundred and ten on that thing. I'm surprised it didn't shake apart."

"It's modified for street racing, Jimmy. She can take that much and more." Rusty patted the motorcycle as he talked.

"Still, at your age-"

"At my age? I'm not even close to being done living, my young friend. And I am always careful of other cars at the turns. If I go, I take only myself."

The officer shook his head. "One of these days, I'm going to be called out here to scrape you up off the pavement. You know that, right?"

"It is at that time you can tell me 'I told you so,'" Rusty replied, giving him a gentle point in the chest.

"Just slow down. For me. Please."

"You got it, Jimmy. I was just about to head home. Tell that beautiful wife and daughter of yours the crazy old Jew says hi."

"Will do," he affirmed as he got into his car. As he drove by Rusty he said. "You are going to have to come for dinner soon. Katie loves those Bible stories."

Rusty waved and replied, "Indeed, I will. Soon."

Once the car was out of sight, Dylan landed and asked, "a friend of yours, huh?"

"You can never have too many friends, Dylan. They are like a badge of honor. The more you have, the bigger the badge."

Dylan shook his head in agreement. "So, the officer said you were nearly at a hundred and ten?"

"I'm glad he was watching. My speedometer doesn't go that high."

"Wow, I was struggling at first but I had a lot left in the tank! I may have been able to double that! What do you think, Hydogall?"

"I think you could have gone maybe three times faster. I knew I could fly fast, but that was me. To my knowledge, this was the first time anyone measured flight speed of a Vessel. Still, I would refrain from flying too fast. Your body, your reflexes are human and not meant for such rigors. If you were to collide with something, even a small bird, at one hundred miles per hour, it would likely kill you."

"Good to know," Dylan said. "I would say higher altitudes would be better, but the air is thinner up there. I might pass out at higher speeds."

They drove back to the cabin. This time Dylan sat in the sidecar. *It really is a smooth ride for such an old piece of machinery,* he thought. Rusty parked the motorcycle in the shop and covered it again. Then he motioned for Dylan to follow him to the work bench.

"All of the prior indwelled Vessels I have known are fireproof. Has Hydogall shared that with you?"

"Yes, a couple of nights ago he told me the story of Dr. Jekyll and Mr. Hyde. The real story, I mean. It was the reason he revealed his spiritual gifts to the doctor," Dylan recounted.

"I would like to hear that story some time. I wasn't sure if you had told him, Hydogall. I know some of the Fallen consider it unsavory or shameful to talk about."

"Indeed, Dr. Carlson," Hydogall confirmed meekly.

Rusty turned and picked up a small plumber's torch. He turned the knob and lit it. It burned deep blue.

"Take off your glove and stick your hand out."

"Wait," Dylan protested. "Can't we start with a match or something?"

"It will not matter," Hydogall stated. "It will not burn your skin."

Dylan reluctantly stuck his hand out slowly. Rusty moved the torch under his flat palm. Starting at a foot below and slowly moving up to the palm. At first, Dylan flinched, not from pain but reflex. As they flame touched his skin, he relaxed.

"I can feel the pressure of the gas and I can tell it's hot, but there is no pain. Not even the smell of burned hair or skin." Dylan removed his hand and looked closely at it. "You can't even tell the flame touched it."

"Just remember," Rusty instructed, putting the torch back on the shelf. "Your clothes are not fireproof. If you walk through fire, you'll come out naked." Rusty chuckled, obviously remembering something he wasn't sharing.

"There is something else I would like you to see," Rusty said. He walked over to the workbench and reached under the side, obviously grabbing something out of sight. He pulled on the workbench and half the wall swiveled out like a giant door.

"Give me a hand with this, my friend," Rusty asked.

Dylan pulled the door back further to reveal a hidden room. The room was eight feet deep and ran the entire width of the building. There were storage racks filled with survival food and equipment all covered with a thick layer of dust. Another rack had firearms and edged weapons along with copious amounts of ammunition.

"I told you I bought this place from a survivalist? Well, this was his hidden supply cache. He left it all here when he moved out."

Dylan picked up a box of survival food. "Cookies," he observed. "Well, it expired last year but I'm sure it's still good given our climate." He walked around the racks, looking at the equipment. "Gas masks, guns, big knives, why would the guy leave it all? This is expensive stuff."

"He was disillusioned with the lifestyle. I'm sure he thought it would sweeten the deal. Or he didn't know what to do with it. All of this equipment was bought off the record. It doesn't exist on any computer or government list. I accepted them, but have not opened the door since we closed escrow."

"I have never fired a gun in my life," Dylan said. "It would probably be more dangerous in my hands than Dagnem's."

"I am not speaking of the firearms, my friend. They would require some service before being operable anyway. There are some other items I believe may be helpful." They spent another hour examining many items to determine their possible usefulness, then Rusty stated, "I think we've done enough for today. Patty will be back soon. Let's go start dinner."

Dylan agreed and they walked back to the cabin. Rusty was barbequing pork ribs for dinner and had been marinating them all day. Rusty fired up the grill and put the ribs on, while Dylan prepared macaroni and cheese and salad.

Soon Patty pulled up in front of the cabin. Dylan saw her grab her purse and a large box from the passenger seat. He walked out to see if he could help her.

"I brought you a gift," she said turning to give him a peck on the cheek. "Nice apron, by the way."

"Thanks," he replied. "What did you get?"

"Oh, just a motorcycle helmet with a Bluetooth headset and microphone."

"Wow, Patty, you shouldn't have done that," Dylan told her, looking closely at the box. "This had to be expensive."

"Oh, it was, but you are worth it, my dear."

"Let me pay you for it."

"Absolutely not! It's a gift, buddy. Take it and use it. And don't give me any guff." She gave him a light punch on the shoulder.

Dylan relented. "This is awesome, Patty. How does it work?"

She showed him how the communication system connected to his cell phone, and there were microphones outside the helmet so you could hear around you while wearing it. Apparently, the microphones blocked loud noises, like wind or engines, but allowed other noises in. Rusty came in and admired it, as well. They plugged it in to charge it for use the next day.

At dinner, Hydogall recounted the events that led to the Jekyll and Hyde book. Rusty and Patty were completely spellbound by the tale.

When he had finished, Patty asked, "so why did the author shorten the name to Hyde instead of Hydogall?"

"Thaddeus Cray was not given to imbibing much, but on this evening, he overindulged a bit. He had changed much of the events as he regaled Mr. Stevenson, but 'Hyde' was an accident. He started to say my name and stopped halfway through, realizing he did not want people knowing who I was. He did not want my name associated with such a bad person. Mr. Stevenson added the 'Mister' to it. I suppose it cemented the duality of the character."

"I am so used to being the story teller, it is a real treat to be a listener. Story telling is such an ancient art form. Perhaps that is why you are so good at it, my friend," Rusty said.

"That is the way knowledge spread for millennia before writing was invented," Hydogall explained. "And even after. Having whole populations that can read is a relatively new concept. I think some things are lost in the translation, at times."

They continued talking over dinner, then moved once again to the porch for dessert. They spoke of the weather and of the upcoming Finals at the University. Rusty decided to change the conversation to more serious matters.

"Hydogall, what can you tell us about Dagnem's abilities?"

"As an Angel of Death, the Father would often have them act on his behalf. He has killed thousands of men, women, even children if needed."

"Children?" Dylan asked.

"It was a brutal time. Civilization was young and the rules were quite literally written in stone. If you did not heed His warning, your entire community could be wiped off the face of the Earth. If you stood against His chosen people, you often did not last long. Dagnem did not enjoy serving the Father, but he enjoyed his work."

"What can Dylan expect the Vessel to be able to do?" Rusty asked.

"He will be as strong as you, as resilient. If the Vessel is naturally stronger, that only adds to it. He will have exceptional night vision. His greatest asset will be the ability to travel from shadow to shadow."

"Shadows?" Dylan asked.

"For him, shadows are like holes in space. He can move into one and come out another anywhere in the vicinity. The shadow only has to be larger than him and he has to be able to see it or to have seen it."

"Wow that is formidable. Can he fly?" Dylan asked.

"No, nor can he become invisible."

"And that is all? No other extraordinary abilities?" Rusty asked.

"Well, when he was alive he had a flaming sword and hands tipped with sharp claws, but he does not possess those now."

They sat together and spoke of strategies for several more hours. They discussed many avenues of attack and defense. When there was a lull in the conversation, Patty asked a difficult question.

"Hydogall, you said before it was a topic you didn't want to discuss, but I was wondering if you would share with us why you were cast out?"

All were silent for a short time, then Hydogall replied, "I do owe you an explanation. The answer goes back to the passage in the Bible that Rusty mentioned earlier. The Book of Genesis, Chapter Six."

Rusty's eyes perked up. "You? You took a human bride?"

"Indeed. You must remember that angels and humans are completely separate types of beings. That is by design. Angels are like caretakers for humans, almost like godparents. It is a sacred duty and our main reason for existing."

"Like robots?" Dylan asked.

"No, we are divine beings who are at the pinnacle of duty. There is no greater service than the direct service to the Father. I have experienced the formation of galaxies, observed the destruction of whole civilizations and even saw the breath of life as it entered Adam's lungs. We are not robots and most are completely fulfilled in their duty."

"It sounds amazing," Patty said.

"My sin was embracing an emotion I had no right to. I fell in love with a young woman I had been observing since before she was born. She was an incredible individual, not beautiful as humans define beauty, but such inner strength and devotion to others. I revealed myself and before long we were married. We were together for five years before the Father acted on my treachery."

"That sounds so harsh. How can love be a sin?" Dylan asked.

"Angels know the purest form of love, Dylan. The love we share with the Father is the definition of fulfillment. Think of the feeling you had when you realized you loved Patty. Or when your mother would sing you to sleep when you were sick. Or even when you eat very fine chocolate. Imagine every form of the emotion humans call love. Now form all those together into one and multiply it times a thousand. That is what the love of the Father feels like."

"Then how could you embrace the love of the woman?" Rusty asked.

"I simply chose to. A flaw in my thinking, I suppose," Hydogall replied.

"But you can't choose who you fall in love with," Dylan offered.

"No, but you can choose what you do about it," Rusty said. "Take it from a man who has fallen in love more times than he can remember."

"Angels have a higher sense of being. I knew exactly what would happen to me as a result of my action, and I did it regardless. I do not regret my experience, as I fully knew what would happen as a result."

"That just seems so sad," Patty chimed in.

"If a husband cheats on his wife or vice versa, is it sad for the cheater? No, it is sad for the one cheated on. I earned my exile. My only true regret is the impact of my actions on the Father. Like any 'parent,' it is not easy to discipline your 'children.' It saddened Him greatly, I'm sure."

"Is there no hope of forgiveness?" Rusty asked.

"No, as I said, angels are not slaves to their emotions as humans are. I knew what I was doing. I would never ask for forgiveness since I would do it again."

"This is an awkward question, but did you have kids?" Patty asked.

"Indeed. I had a son and a daughter."

"That must have made it even harder," Dylan said.

"At first, I would agree. However, the silver lining was that they were Vessels as were their offspring. I indwelled my own family line for many centuries."

"That kinda sounds gross," Patty grimaced.

Hydogall chuckled. "No, it really was not. Although I have to admit I never indwelled my daughter. I was with my son until he died. Then I moved to my grandson. They visited my daughter's family many times. It is a unique gift to be able to see your blood line grow and flourish."

"Why did you stop indwelling them?" Rusty asked.

"The family grew and spread until I could no longer keep track of them all. Over time, the branch of the family I was indwelling was wiped out in a volcanic eruption in 79AD."

Rusty's eyes perked up. "Pompeii? You were in Pompeii when Vesuvius erupted? That must have been incredible. The entire middle east shook with that one!"

"That eruption was the most energy I had observed being released since the formation of the planet. However, my Vessel at the time, a very distant grandson, was killed within seconds of the first explosion. There was not time to take it all in thoroughly before I returned to Hell."

All were silent for a few moments, then Rusty spoke, "well, it has been a long day. I'm heading up to bed. If you are okay with it, I would like to have a small service in the morning, since it is Sunday. Nothing formal, just Communion, a few songs and a short devotional. I don't like to miss my Worship time."

"Sure, Rusty. We look forward to it," Patty said.

Chapter 8 – Close to Home

The morning brought a short service in Rusty's living room. Dylan was not 100% comfortable with a Worship service, but he had accompanied Patty a few times to her local congregation and understood what was happening. Still, he had never attended a service so intimate. He usually talked Patty into sitting in the back.

Perhaps sensing his unease, Rusty made sure the service was over in an hour. Since Dylan did not know the words to the hymns, he asked Hydogall if he would like to sing, which he did with glee. Angels, it seems, only had one volume when singing the Father's praises, and it is loud. Hydogall also asked if he might take Communion and Dylan was fine with it.

When they finished up the service, they ate a quick breakfast of bagels and decided to start cleaning up. Patty took the kitchen area, Dylan the living area and Rusty went outside to lock up the shop. Soon, Dylan joined Patty in the kitchen as she was finishing up.

"So, Dylan," she asked. "How does it feel for a scientist to have 100% verification that there is a god and it is the Biblical God?"

"I don't know what to think, frankly," Dylan replied. "I was never the anti-religion-type of scientist. I saw people of faith doing really great things in the name of religion while my peers tended to focus on the not so great things. Gazing out at the universe as much as I have, I just kinda figured there had to be something greater out there. How about you? You have always been a faithful person. How does it feel to have that faith confirmed?"

"Smug as heck," she chuckled. "Just kidding, it does feel nice though, but I didn't need it. Do you feel like it's maybe time to start focusing a little more on that faithful side?"

119

Dylan thought a moment. "I guess it is, but this is all so overwhelming right now. I will definitely be looking closer at it soon."

Patty furrowed her brow a bit. "Hydogall, what happens to you if Dylan gets baptized? Will you go back to Hell?"

"I may stay if Dylan allows it," Hydogall said. "The Fallen may only indwell a baptized adult if they have full consent. That is how I was able to move to Thaddeus Cray."

"Thaddeus was a religious man?" Dylan asked.

"Very," Hydogall replied.

They finished up and went upstairs to quickly pack. Since they hadn't brought much, they were soon done and back downstairs. Rusty had come in and grabbed a few things from the fridge to take home. They locked up and headed to their cars. Rusty pulled out first, waving as he drove off. Patty and Dylan pulled away next, heading down the short dirt road which lead to the highway.

They dropped Patty's things off at her house first since they planned to spend the rest of the day together. Then they went to Dylan's place and dropped his things off. Once there, they decided to go for a walk around the neighborhood.

The tree-lined streets of Laramie were beautiful this time of year. Many of the homes and trees were over a century old. The uneven sidewalk had to be half that. The birds were singing and the air was clean. They walked for a long time, holding hands and talking about everything except angels and demons. This was a typical Sunday afternoon for them, and they were enjoying it.

They ate an early dinner together at a small restaurant downtown. They visited the local shops and Dylan picked up a burner cell phone to be used with the helmet. Before long, they decided to call it a night. Both had papers to grade for the week and they parted with a kiss at Patty's house. Dylan walked home in the cooling night air. He had forgotten his jacket and rubbed his exposed arms. He took out his phone and checked the temperature.

"Sixty-five degrees?" he questioned under his breath. It felt at least twenty degrees cooler. He was walking by a large park where people were still milling about, walking their dogs, playing with their kids or just hanging out. As he walked along the sidewalk, it felt as if he was getting even colder. After a few minutes, the chill began to subside.

He stopped and looked around. There was no wind. He looked back where he had just been walking. There appeared to be a small impromptu soccer match going on with some young children and their parents, but nothing to explain the chill.

Then it dawned on him the chill wasn't in his exposed arms, it was running up his spine. *Could this be the feeling Rusty was talking about,* he thought.

"Hydogall," he said quietly. "Is he here?"

"I believe he is near, Dylan," Hydogall replied.

"There are dozens of people out here. Is there any way of knowing which one is him?"

"Look for someone out of place. According to news reports, the murders began in southern Colorado. The Vessel is likely not from Wyoming."

"So, he probably wouldn't think to have a jacket with him. Of course, neither do I."

"It is a start, Dylan. Also, I would suggest walking behind that stand of short trees and becoming invisible. If he is here, he felt your presence, too. If you are walking around obviously on the hunt, he may see you first. Anonymity is your greatest strength right now."

121

Dylan walked behind the trees and become invisible. He also took to the air twenty feet to get a better view. He hovered over the soccer game, trying to get the chill to return.

"Dylan, there is a black sedan parked across the street. It has a New Mexico license plate," Hydogall pointed out.

Dylan moved over towards the car. As he did, the car suddenly started and began to pull away.

"That's suspicious," Dylan replied. He began to pursue the vehicle when he was suddenly hit very hard in the back of the head. It jarred him and he saw stars for a few seconds. Then he heard gasps from below.

"Dylan, you are visible!" Hydogall stated a little louder than usual.

Dylan became invisible again and quickly flew to another part of the park, but still hung in the air. He rubbed his head vigorously.

"What hit me?" he asked.

"I believe it was the soccer ball. You were hovering over the game and I noticed it bouncing away as we departed."

"Stupid rookie mistake," he said. "How many people do you think saw me?"

"There were twenty-three people in the immediate area, ten of whom were children. Three adults were using their cell phones to record their children. I am sure at least one got you on the recording, but they were all behind you and likely did not get your face."

"Laramie's a small town, Hydogall," Dylan said. "Let's hope nobody got a good look or a good recording of my face. Do you see the black car?"

"I do not. Perhaps if you fly higher over the area, we can see more?"

Dylan flew high up into the air, but the trees were too thick. He decided to head home and get some work done. There was no use worrying about anything yet.

He flew to his house. It was a different perspective in the air. He found himself flying above the same streets he would be walking or driving along to get home. He cut over a few blocks of houses to his small backyard. Taking a look around and seeing no one, he entered through the back door and became visible.

He spent the next few hours reading student papers. He had promised them he would have them graded by Monday morning's class. When he finished, he opened up his tablet to see if anyone had posted video of him to social media.

Unfortunately, there were two videos posted. Both showed him appear suddenly when the soccer ball hit him. He was visible for less than five seconds and all you could see was his clothes and hair color. It wasn't even obvious if he was a male or a short-haired female. You couldn't really even tell the ethnicity. Still, maybe he would wear a hat for a few days or at least get a haircut.

The internet was abuzz with the video regardless of how brief his appearance was. Most believed it to be a hoax. However, the locals who had been there and had seen it with their own eyes were plentiful. Despite Hydogall's assertion that only twenty-three people had been in the area, more than fifty now claimed to have seen him appear. Many were flakes, with one saying he looked like the Mothman. Still, some were legitimate and this would be a major local story for some time. Luckily, the national news hadn't picked up the story just yet.

Dylan didn't know what to do. The element of surprise wasn't completely gone, since no one knew who he was, but Dagnem certainly now knew that Hydogall had revealed himself to his Vessel. That would make things harder.

Dylan decided that surprise was exactly what was required. He needed to take the fight to Dagnem. He went to his closet and picked out his training clothes. He dressed, leaving his wallet and keys on his dresser. He used his burner phone to connect to his helmet and checked the connection. He put the helmet on then used a rag to wipe it clean of fingerprints. Using the same rag, he wiped the phone before securing it in the inside pocket of his leather jacket. Last, he put on his gloves and boots. He made sure that there was nothing he wore that could be traced back to him.

He became invisible and crept out the back door, making sure there was no one watching. As he rose in the air, he remembered to close the helmet's visor. This was the first time he had flown with it on, and it was odd at first. So big and bulky. *Maybe some type of neck roll would be helpful,* he thought. It also took a few minutes to get used to hearing through the earphones, but he got used to it.

As he flew slowly towards downtown, Dylan was glad to see an obvious police presence. *Two murders in a small town linked to a serial killer will do that,* he thought. The moon was high, giving him a pretty unobstructed view from a hundred feet above town. He crisscrossed the downtown area, searching for a black sedan. He saw a few, but none with New Mexico plates.

Suddenly he heard some loud voices coming from the front of a bar. Two men were obviously close to blows over who knew what. Both men slurred their speech as they yelled, and both had women holding them back.

Dylan, still invisible, dropped down between them, pushing them away. He shouted loudly, "Listen to the girls! Back off!" Unfortunately, his visor was down so it was louder to his ears than to theirs. Both men stumbled back against their dates with funny looks on their faces. Dylan raised his visor, still invisible, and spoke slowly and loudly, "go home now!" This time, all four stumbled back and

124

began to run in opposite directions. "And let the ladies drive!" He called even louder.

Dylan smiled and went back up into the air. He left the visor open this time, since he wasn't flying very fast. There was no black sedan to be found and he wasn't feeling the chill up his spine, either. He followed 3rd Street south to the edge of town where it crossed over I-80. He noticed a car pulled over on the side of the Interstate. It wasn't a black sedan, but was out of place. He flew over and descended for a better view.

The car was older and had a few dents, but the biggest issue it had was a flat tire on the rear passenger side. There was an elderly woman trying to get the spare tire out of the trunk.

Dylan landed a hundred feet behind her and made himself visible. There was scant traffic this time of night so he knew he wouldn't be noticed. He opened his visor and asked, "need some help, ma'am?"

The woman jumped slightly and turned to face him, squinting.

"Just a flat, young man. I can handle it," she said in typical Wyoming self-reliant fashion.

"Please, allow me to help. What kind of man allows a lady to change her own tire?"

The woman narrowed her eyes at him. "Where'd you come from, buddy?"

"My bike is parked just back down the road. I had stopped to stretch my legs when you passed me."

She looked over his shoulder where he had come from. "I guess I didn't see you."

"My fault. I had my bike shut off so my lights weren't on."

"Lucky I didn't run you over."

"Yes, ma'am. Now let's get that tire changed." Dylan retrieved the spare and the jack from the trunk and spent the next few minutes changing the tire and listening to the woman's story. She had been spending the weekend in Laramie with her sister and was on her way back to Cheyenne. They had wanted to do a girl's weekend for such a long time. She was sure her husband had 'probably been living on pizza' for the last two days and the house would be a mess, but it was worth it.

Dylan packed the jack and flat tire into the trunk. The lady shook his hand and thanked him.

"You're not from Wyoming, are you son?" she asked.

"No ma'am, northern California, actually. But I work here now."

"California, huh? Well, good to see Wyoming is wearing off on you."

"It is fast becoming my favorite place in the world, ma'am."

They parted and the woman gave him another quick wave as she pulled away. Dylan looked around and, seeing no one, took to the air, becoming invisible. He wondered if he should follow her home but decided she really didn't need his help. She had a cell phone and the service was good for the fifty-mile trip. Besides, he wasn't done looking for the sedan.

He flew back towards town, arcing east towards the Walmart supercenter. It was a beacon at night with its brightly lit parking lot. Still no black sedan. He flew over all the hotel and motel parking lots. No black sedan. After an hour more, he gave up and flew home.

Landing in his backyard, he scanned the area and went in the back door, becoming visible as he stepped in. He pulled a large, empty suitcase out of his hall closet and began to pack all his clothes, boots, gloves and helmet. They fit inside perfectly. He placed the suitcase back into the closet.

He placed the burner phone on the charger and completed his nightly routine. Before long he was lying in bed.

"Hydogall?" he asked.

"Yes, Dylan?"

"What is heaven like?"

"Indescribable," Hydogall replied.

"Really? You can't give me anything? Are there people walking golden streets? Is my old dog there?" Anything?"

"Golden streets are a metaphor, Dylan. It is another plane of existence where people are always happy. They are completely fulfilled. No pain, no anger, no displeasure at all."

"Sounds nice," Dylan said, yawning.

"It is," Hydogall replied.

Dylan wanted to ask more questions, but the events of the last three days were wearing on him. He closed his eyes and before long was sound asleep.

***

Two blocks north of Dylan, the man indwelling Dagnem sat on a screened porch, sipping brandy and smoking a cigar. His car was neatly stowed in the detached garage behind the house. Inside the house, the former occupant lay near the front door, a fist-sized hole where his heart should have been.

He glanced over to the corner of the backyard where the dead man's wife had been hastily buried five years prior after she found child pornography on his computer. The dead man had built a shed over it in hopes of concealing his deed. Unfortunately for him, Dagnem had only to gaze into his eyes to see his worst sins. *This house will work for a few days*, he thought. He had felt Hydogall's presence at the park and the videos he had seen on the news proved it. Hydogall had seen his car, so he would keep it hidden and borrow the dead man's car. It wasn't very luxurious, but it would work for now.

***

The next morning, Dylan woke and ran through his morning routine. His only deviation was when he stopped near the hall trying to decide if he should take something with him. His helmet? His leather jacket? He decided not to bring anything. He could, after all, turn invisible if he needed to do anything. Either he carried it all or he carried nothing.

He caught his bus and gave a quick hello to Sam, the driver. Today he sat near the front and chatted with Sam as they drove. It wasn't a long drive, but he did get to know Sam a lot better. It turned out Sam was quite the talker once you engaged him. In the short drive, Dylan got Sam's life story and what an interesting story it was.

Entering his building, he encountered Neville and they had their normal morning exchange. He noticed the building felt even colder than usual, so he hurried up the stairs to his office.

What he neglected to see was the man sitting in the corner reading the newspaper. The man noticed Dylan and from behind his paper stared deeply. When Dylan went up the stairs, the man indwelling Dagnem stood up and walked over to Neville, who was getting his backpack on.

"Excuse me, Corporal?" he asked remembering what Dylan had called him.

Neville took his ever-present headphones off and stood at a salute. The man returned it and Neville relaxed.

"Could you tell me who that man was that just came in?"

"That was Mr. Mathis. He tells me to call him Dylan, but I don't. He works on the second floor. He's an Astrology professor."

"Astrology?"

"Yeah, you know, stars and planets and stuff. Astrology."

"Oh, okay. Thank you, Corporal."

Neville saluted again, then started towards the door and the waiting bus he could see outside. To the side of the room was a student computer lab. The man walked into the lab and found an open computer. It required no log-in information and he began to search the internet for any information on Dr. Dylan Mathis of Laramie, Wyoming.

He found many publications and pictures of him and his colleagues at workshops and conventions. He could not find an address except the one for the College. However, when scanning the pictures, he noticed the same woman with him in quite a few. One of the captions read, 'Dr. Dylan Mathis and Patricia Nielsohn, PhD candidate at Bridger Community College." *Was she a love interest?* He thought. The side hug they shared seemed a little more intimate than colleagues. He searched for information on Patricia Nielsohn and found her office on campus.

Chapter 9 – Make Ready

Dylan spent the rest of his day as he normally did. He taught his class, had his office time and researched the recorded celestial data from the weekend. It was nearly five o'clock when he heard a knock at his open door.

Rusty walked in with a slight smile on his face. "How are you feeling today, my friend?"

"Pretty good. I was a little sore yesterday, but that's gone now."

"Good, good," he replied. "So, it's probably a good idea to go out tonight, you think?"

"I actually went out last night," Dylan replied matter-of-factly.

"Really?" Rusty asked, obviously surprised.

"I wanted to try out everything. Sunday night in Laramie is pretty slow. I stopped a fight, helped an old lady change her tire. That's pretty much it."

"Well, this isn't a big city. Not a large criminal element here. A hero does what he can." Rusty smiled big after saying the word 'hero.' "I saw the video online. Sounds like most people are writing it off as a hoax. Not the locals, though."

"And I doubt Dagnem will either. I blew it. He knows Hydogall and I are working together."

"True, but he still doesn't know who you are, my friend."

"So, we still have some element of surprise, I suppose."

"What did Patty say about the video?"

"You know, I haven't talked to her all day. I texted her a couple of times, but she never replied. I'm sure her Master Professor is keeping her busy. It's almost time for Finals."

"Still, in a time like this, it is a little odd her not checking her messages."

"That's Patty," Dylan quipped. "I'll try her again." Dylan sent her a text and they waited. After a few minutes, he called her and she didn't answer. He called her desk phone and still no answer. "Maybe we should go by her office," Dylan stated.

He and Rusty hurried downstairs and quickly crossed over to the building where she had her small office. She wasn't there but her door was open. The light was off, so Dylan turned it on. Everything looked like it should. He asked the guy in the office next door if he had seen her and he replied that she was there this morning but he hadn't seen her in hours.

"She doesn't leave her door open, Rusty. Like ever."

"Maybe you should go over to her house. I'll look for her car. You can go faster without me, if you get my meaning."

Rusty hurried down stairs while Dylan ran upstairs. As he neared the roof access, he became invisible. He opened the door quickly, scaring three smoking undergrads in the process. He quickly took to the air and headed towards Patty's house.

"I'm worried, Hydogall," he said.

"I am also," Hydogall replied. "It is unlike Dagnem to do anything during the day with so few shadows, but her absence is more than curious."

Dylan landed in Patty's backyard, took a quick glance around and became visible. Patty always locked her doors, even when she was home. Luckily, Dylan had the key. He opened the backdoor and cried out, "Patty?"

There was no reply. He moved from room to room through the small house and Patty was nowhere to be found. Nothing seemed amiss. Her car was not in the driveway.

He called Rusty who answered immediately. "I found her car in the parking lot," Rusty noted. "Nothing out of place."

"I'm at her house and everything looks fine. I'll meet you back at my office."

"Okay, my friend. Don't worry, I'm sure everything is fine."

Dylan flew back to campus and landed on the roof of his building. He became visible and walked inside and down the stairs to his office floor. Rusty was waiting for him outside his door and they both went in. Rusty closed the door behind him.

"This is weird," Dylan said.

"Indeed. I happened by her Master Professor and she said Patty was in her office this morning but she had not seen her in a while. No classes to teach, no projects to grade."

Suddenly Dylan's phone rang. Dylan looked at the screen and burst out, "it's her!" He hit the speaker button so Rusty could hear. "Hey sweetie! We've been looking all over for you!"

It was not Patty's voice that answered. "Patty has been spending the day with me, Dylan," answered the deep voice of an older man.

Dylan's heart sank and his head felt ready to explode. "Who is this?" he asked shakily. Rusty moved to shut the door.

"I have had many names, but you may call me Dagnem."

"What have you done with Patty?" Rusty asked forcefully.

"We have been spending time together, as I said. I have not harmed a single hair on her head, so far."

"Let me speak to her!" Dylan yelled.

"Of course, I am not a monster." There was the sound of the phone being shifted around.

"Dylan!" It was Patty's voice.

"Patty, are you okay?" Dylan screamed in the phone.

"I'm okay! He came to my office. Grabbed me. Pulled me behind the door and suddenly we were in a dark room! I don't know…" She was cut off.

"Patty!"

"It is very simple, Hydogall. Instead of killing her, I want to kill you. Believe it or not, I don't relish the thought of killing her. Her sins are few, but they are sins so I could punish her and still be righteous."

"You have never been righteous, coward!" yelled Hydogall.

"There you are, Brother. I am so happy to hear you. I am so looking forward to reacquainting you with Hell. Do you remember it, Hydogall? I do. It is still *very* fresh in my mind."

"Evil deserves to lie in its own filth, Dagnem. Hell was created for creatures such as you."

"Creatures such as us, Hydogall. Your residency was established as much as mine. Or do you think the Father made a mistake? Oh, Brother, you have been gone far too long."

"What is it that you want us to do, Dagnem?" Hydogall asked, frustrated.

"Your tenure on this plane of existence ends today. You will face me or this poor, pathetic female dies a rather agonizing death."

"If you hurt her…" Dylan spat out.

"Listen to your Vessel, Hydogall. Will he make me pay? Will I rue the day? Oh, these hairless chimps and their empty threats."

Dylan shook with fear and anger. He struggled to steady his voice. "Fine. Where do you want to meet us?"

"Us? Oh, that is so sweet. You have embraced your 'squatter.' At sundown, meet me at the train yard. How is that for dramatic, monkey?"

"And you'll have Patty with you?"

"Absolutely. And not a hair will be harmed." With that, the phone hung up.

Dylan turned to Rusty. "We need a plan."

"I have one," Rusty replied.

The air was crisp as Dylan flew imperceptibly towards the train yard. After Rusty discussed his plan, Dylan had gone home to get his gear. As he approached, he could see the dozens of trains parked there. It wasn't completely private, but more so than anywhere else in town. The area was illuminated by bright overhead spotlights casting a multitude of shadows. A perfect setting for Dagnem.

Dagnem came into view between two rows of train cars. He stood with his arms casually folded behind him. He was an unassuming man, maybe forty, dressed in a short trench coat, a t-shirt and jeans. Unsurprisingly, Patty was not there. As Dylan descended fifty feet from Dagnem, he shouted, "where is Patty?"

Dagnem searched the dark sky. "Oh, she is here, just not in sight. I could not have you swooping in and grabbing her, then flying off. Rest assured, she is here and once you are dead, I will release her."

"Because your word means so much," Dylan replied.

***

Unknown to Dagnem, Rusty was two cars behind him. He crept slowly along the tracks, listening to their exchange. In his arms, he carried a 12-guage shotgun loaded with slugs. His primary goal was to backup Dylan, but now that Patty wasn't in view, he had to switch tactics.

***

"Dylan, you are going to have to keep him busy while I search for Patty. Remember your training," Rusty whispered into his wireless headset

"Understood," Dylan replied quietly into his helmet mike.

"I have waited over a hundred years for this, Hydogall!" Dagnem yelled. "Show yourself!"

"Dylan landed softly and became visible. "Here I am, murderer!" Hydogall yelled back.

"Nice outfit," Dagnem observed. "Tell me, is that jacket supposed to be some sort of armor?" With that, Dagnem drew his hands around so Dylan could see them. On his right hand was a shiny metal gauntlet with sharp studs that ran up to his elbow. At its fingertips were long, pointed spikes. "I may not have my own claws, but my Vessel was a very good metal worker."

"What do you mean 'was'?" Dylan asked.

"Well, he was a capable killer in his own right, but when he found out what I could do, he voluntarily allowed me to take charge. Now he just watches as I do the work. Occasionally he chimes in, but only when I let him."

"That's a thing?" he said to himself.

"Yes, a Vessel may surrender control of their body to the Fallen. However, they can only take control again if the Fallen in turn surrenders control. Very few Vessels would ever do that."

"He is not a normal person. He lives for the kill and I am very efficient at it. And he still gets to experience it all. Am I correct, Sven?"

"Absolutely!" said a different, higher pitched voice coming from Dagnem.

Behind Dagnem, Dylan spotted Rusty slowly moving from car to car, searching for Patty. Most of the cars were open on the side and he could see inside easily. For others he was listening through the wall for breathing or movement. Dylan knew if Rusty slid any doors open, the sound would likely alert Dagnem.

"Get on your knees, Hydogall."

"There is no need for this, Dagnem. I will leave my Vessel willingly and return to Hell."

"And how will I know that you will stay there, Brother? You could leave and return in five minutes, since you know him. I would not easily be able to tell if you were there or not. No, the only way to be sure you cannot return is to kill the Vessel. It has to be that way."

"You know he cannot just let you murder him. That is tantamount to suicide, a very serious sin."

"I see your point, however I can see his sins from here. He is not protected, so it will matter little. His fate is already sealed."

"But I cannot allow that fate, Dagnem. That would be my sin. Now, Dylan!" Suddenly Dylan became invisible. He arose above the ground just enough to not leave tracks in the gravel beneath his feet. "You are going to have to work for it, Brother," Hydogall said.

"I guess that is more sporting," Dagnem mused, pulling off his trench coat and exposing dozens of knives in sheaths strapped to his sides. He grabbed one with each hand and threw them in Dylan's direction. Dylan had to dodge very quickly to avoid them and bumped into a train car. When he looked back at Dagnem, he was lighting something, which he quickly threw Dylan's way. The round ball hit the ground and smoke began billowing out. As Dylan stared in confusion, four more smoke bombs hit the ground around Dagnem. The air was filled with thick smoke that hung there in the abnormally still evening. Dagnem scanned his eyes back and forth until they settled on Dylan.

"He can see us in the smoke!" Dylan yelled as one of Dagnem's knives sliced through his left arm. Dylan yelled in pain and ascended above the smoke, a trail behind him.

Dagnem walked over to the car nearest him and reached into the shadow. He pulled his hand back and showed he had Patty by the back of the head, her body still in the shadow. Her mouth was gagged and her eyes, puffy from crying, showed true terror. "She is waiting for you!" Dagnem yelled into the air. He shoved her hard back into the shadow.

"No!" Dylan yelled, diving through the smoke straight at Dagnem. His speed was something neither expected and the two collided hard. Both men sprawled out on the asphalt between the cars.

***

Meanwhile, Rusty was still searching for Patty when he heard a loud clang. When Dagnem pushed Patty back into the shadow, her chair fell over in the car she was stashed in. Rusty ran to the car and, as quietly as he could, slid open the side door. Patty lay on the floor tied to a chair. He jumped inside the car and untied her. She was a little stunned from falling over but quickly recovered and the two exited the car and ran towards downtown.

***

"I have her, my friend!" Rusty stage whispered into his wireless headset. "I am taking her to my car. Get out of there!"

Dylan heard the message but had trouble making his body do what he wanted it to. The impact had knocked the wind out of him. He glanced around and didn't see Dagnem. He slowly took to the air, oblivious that he was visible.

***

Rusty opened the door to his car and helped Patty sit inside. He ran around the back of the vehicle to the driver side. Suddenly he was grabbed by the legs and was pulled down. He grabbed at the asphalt but was yanked under the car.

When he hit the ground again, he was on top of a building and Dagnem stood next to him. He was bleeding profusely from his forehead. Dagnem picked him up by the back of the neck then looked around. Seeing Dylan in the distance, he yelled, "Hydogall, this is yet another human you have failed!" With that, he plunged the sharp points of the gauntlet into Rusty's chest.

Dylan screamed, "NO!" as he flew quickly towards them. Dagnem, again not expecting Dylan's speed, dove into a nearby shadow. Dylan landed on the roof at a run and slid next to Rusty. He grabbed him hard, bringing him up to his lap where he heard two soft words, "my friend…" and then Rusty was gone.

Chapter 10 – Flight or Fight?

It was a large memorial. Rusty had been a fixture in Laramie for many years and touched a lot of lives. The service had to be held in the college gymnasium to accommodate everyone who wished to attend, and still some people were standing.

Dylan had placed Rusty's body in his car. He then placed an anonymous call to the police on his burner phone saying he saw something going on at the train yard and Rusty's body was soon discovered. His autopsy was hurried and he was deemed yet another victim of the serial killer.

His only known relative was a niece who quickly made her way to town. She made all the arrangements and in accordance with his family's tradition, Rusty was buried at his family's plot in Israel.

Dylan and Patty had been staying in a hotel room in Laramie. They had purchased enough lamps and flashlights to be sure there were no shadows anywhere in the room. They knew he had to have been there before to use them, but they couldn't take the risk. It helped them sleep, knowing Hydogall never slept and could hear anything in the room when they closed their eyes.

Both had been given leave at work. Being near the end of the semester, it wasn't hard to find people willing to finish out their courses for them. The College had cancelled classes for a few days after Rusty's death to increase security. There were only a few weeks of class left to cover.

After Rusty's memorial service, Dylan and Patty began walking to her car. Rusty's niece hurried over to catch them. She was a young woman, maybe in her thirties and was unaccompanied.

"Excuse me, are you by chance Dylan and Patty?" she asked.

"Yeah," Dylan replied, sticking out his hand.

"We haven't met. I'm Rusty's niece, Martha." She took Dylan's hand into hers. Instead of shaking it, she grabbed it with the both hands and squeezed softly.

"It's nice to meet you, Martha. I'm so sorry for your loss," Dylan consoled.

"Thank you. Uncle Rusty obviously meant as much to you as he did to me. Judging from the size of the service, he meant a lot to this town, too."

"Yeah, he had a lot of friends," Patty replied.

"I'm not surprised. He makes friends wherever he goes," she said looking back at the lowering casket. "Uncle Rusty was very fond of you two. I just spoke with him last week and he mentioned you by name. You must have meant a lot to him."

"He meant a lot to us, too. He was a terrific person and a great friend," Dylan lamented.

"I'm going to be in town a few days settling his affairs. I do have a copy of his Will and I know there are a few items he wanted you to have. I'll get with his lawyer and set everything up later this week."

"Sounds good," Dylan agreed.

"There is one other thing. When I went by his house, I found this note addressed to you. I'm not sure what's in it, but I thought I would drop it with you when I saw you." She handed the envelope to Dylan.

"Thank you," Dylan said.

"Well, I'm going to get going. There is so much to do. Thank you again for being a good friend to my uncle." She gave each of them a hug and walked away.

Dylan and Patty walked to her car. As they got in, Dylan opened the sealed envelope bearing his name and read it aloud.

"Dylan and Patty, if you are reading this, something went wrong tonight and I didn't make it. As you can see, I was worried something might go awry. I have lived a very long life and as you know I have experienced more than any one person should be able to. Please, do not grieve long for me. Mine was not a life lived in vain. I traveled the world and met many people. They are my legacy, as are you. I believe the Father has a plan for us all and while my time is finally up, yours has only begun. The lives you touch now will be *your* legacy. Though the night seems dark now, dawn will come eventually and the light of Love and Truth will shine. I hope to see you again someday, though not anytime soon. Your friend, Rusty."

Dylan smiled. "He drew a smiley face after 'soon'." Patty laughed.

They hugged through their tears. They drove to a coffee shop and sat in a booth to talk. Patty looked around to make sure no one was within earshot.

"We need a plan, Dylan," she said, a serious tone to her voice.

"Well, first I'm going to take you to my sister's apartment in Fort Collins."

"What? You're not getting rid of me!"

"No, I'm protecting you. He knows who you are and could try and attack you again. I already arranged it with Melanie. She can't wait to see you."

Patty thought for a minute. "Okay, I get it. I'm a liability as long as he can use me to get to you. That doesn't make it right. I can hide…"

Dylan interrupted her. "The only way I can know you are safe is if you are not here."

"If he knows about you, he could know about Melanie. We may be in just as much trouble together."

"That's why you and Melanie are spending the next week in Vail. My treat. She is making the arrangements so I won't even know where you are. We're leaving right after we stop and pick up some clothes for you."

They sat silent for a moment. Then Patty asked, "Hydogall, are we doing the right thing?"

"Yes, Patty, I believe you are. Dylan and I have spoken about this at length and it was my suggestion to go to Colorado. It is highly unlikely Dagnem would be able to find you there."

"Why do you think he hasn't attacked again?" she asked.

"Dagnem knows that we are watching for him. He has to make a new plan of attack. On top of that, he undoubtedly likes knowing we are in fear until his next attack. He is sadistic by nature. Hell does that to some."

They finished their coffee and drove back to the hotel to retrieve their things. They next drove to Patty's house so she could pack for the long trip. Dylan had gone there the day after Rusty was killed and locked everything up tightly. Still, he entered first and looked around as he turned every light on. Not feeling Dagnem's presence, he brought Patty inside and she packed. She filled a large suitcase and they were soon back of the road. As they drove through Laramie, they noticed there was a heavy police and FBI presence in town. They headed south for the hour and a half trip to Fort Collins.

142

They were silent for a long time, which was uncharacteristic for either of them on a car trip. Dylan stared straight ahead while Patty stared out the window into the distance. Suddenly, Patty turned to Dylan.

"Hydogall?" she asked.

"Yes, Patty," Hydogall replied.

"How did you and Thaddeus Cray kill Dagnem's last Vessel?"

"That is an interesting story, Patty."

***

Whitechapel Parish, London 1889

Thaddeus Cray was nearing his 50th birthday. As his housekeeper served him breakfast on his balcony, he looked out at the city. Though he lived in an area beneath his station, he was told, the views were exquisite on clear days.

His housekeeper, Mrs. Eberhardt, who was the large flats only other occupant, was used to hearing Thaddeus talk to himself as he sat alone. She had served him long enough that he often didn't even stop talking when she entered the room. She thought him eccentric, but a very fine master.

Thaddeus was smiling even more than usual this April morning. After a lifetime of bachelorhood, he had finally met a woman he could settle down with. All of these years he had made a conscious effort not to get involved with anyone due to a voracious workload and in some small part due to his role as a Vessel for the Fallen Angel, Hydogall. He doubted any woman could be happy with a man that so openly spoke to himself, but he and Hydogall were friends, and he could not deny his presence, at least not in the privacy of his own home.

Then came Mary Kelly. She was an unfortunate woman who had had a storied past after her young husband died in a mining

143

accident in Ireland. She had come to London still rather young herself and, finding no work, took some unsavory jobs to make ends meet. In was in that capacity they had met. Thaddeus often took *pro bono* cases to help the poor when he wasn't representing London's elite. He had helped Mary stay out of prison and offered her a job as his laundress. He soon found he was taking her his laundry nearly every day, just for her company. She was half his age, but her struggles seemingly had made her wise beyond her years and fortunately had not dampened her striking physical characteristics.

After two months of making excuses to visit her regularly, he would ask her to marry him this evening. He had asked her to come by his flat to drop off the laundry and even gave her money for a Hansom cab. Judging from her reaction when he visited, he was sure she was as smitten with him as he was with her. He was sure she would agree to marry him and since neither had any close family, they could be wed by the Justice of the Peace on Friday.

He finished his breakfast and readied himself. He had a full day at the office. His practice was very successful and over the years, he had taken on two junior partners whose work and character were admirable. Once married, he would take a long vacation with Mary, perhaps to Ireland to see her family, and leave them in charge of the office.

The day dragged on for Thaddeus. He had twice gone for a walk around the square just to move his feet. He was having trouble focusing on his work, which wasn't like him at all. Finally, at 3:15, he could sit no longer. He left the office and decided to walk home the long way. He stopped to chat every now and then with neighborhood folk he was accustomed with, which seemed to be just about everyone. He was well-known and well-liked by every shopkeeper and Bobbie on the street. He had personally helped many of them legally, or even financially at times.

144

Since he had already purchased a ring and had it in his pocket, he stopped to buy some roses. They were Mary's favorite flower and he had brought them to her a few times in the past, under the guise that a client had sent them to him and he had no use for them. He walked along with a spring in his step and a whistle on his lips.

As he was passing a tavern, he happened a glance inside and saw Mary. She was standing next to a gentleman at the bar. Thaddeus was surprised to see her there since she said she had no use for those establishments anymore. He watched as she drank and flirted with the man. Then they left together, laughing and singing an Irish ditty.

Thaddeus was heartbroken. He threw the roses into the bin and stormed down the sidewalk. Mary had not given up her unsavory lifestyle at all. *It was all a ruse,* he thought. *A ruse to get me to fall for her. For what? Money? Sport! What a fool I have been!*

He walked home quickly. Entering the residence, Mrs. Eberhardt remarked that he was never home so early. He walked into his den and closed the door, asking not to be disturbed. He sat in his comfortable chair, looking at the ring he had bought her. He wept openly. Hydogall was silent, words failing him.

A few hours later, there was a knock at the door. Mrs. Eberhardt remarked that 'Mary was here with the laundry' and asked if he would like to see her?

He replied to show her in. Mrs. Eberhardt opened the door and Mary walked in with her bundle of laundry. She smiled as she saw him. Thaddeus did not return the countenance.

"Please have a seat, Mary," he said pointing to the chair across from him.

"Thank you, Sir," she replied.

Thaddeus stood and loped around the room as he spoke. "Mary, I have a confession. I have been in love with you for some time. I can't explain fully why, but you have quite taken me aback. I think of you more and more throughout the day and often can think of nothing else."

Mary's face brightened. "I must confess, Sir, I have similar feelings. I'd hoped you—"

"Imagine my surprise when I came across you having a gay old time in a tavern today before leaving with some rascal out the back door."

Mary's face went pale. She bowed her head and looked at her feet.

"Ah, I see you won't bother to deny it. You told me you had left all that behind. You were doing honest work. I thought we had something. How could you do this to me? To us?"

Mary replied meekly, "I had...expenses, Mr. Cray. Something I had to buy. It's the only way a girl can make fast money in London. I'm...sorry." She began to cry and buried her face in her hands.

"I'm sorry, too. Sorry I could not see the type of person you actually are. I had every intention of proposing marriage to you this very night! Now, I can't stand the sight of you. I want you to leave this flat. Leave and never return. You are free to go do your filthy business unfettered. Be sure that I will not sully your doorstep ever again!"

Mary tried to compose herself. She stood and walked towards the door. "I am sorry, Mr. Cray, Sir. This is not what I wanted of you." She glanced at the bundle of laundry. "Please, don't let the laundry sit too long. It will wrinkle."

Thaddeus motioned to the door. "Mrs. Eberhardt will pay you on the way out. Good day!"

146

Mary stoically walked out the door of the den and within a few moments Thaddeus heard the front door slam. It sounded as if Mrs. Eberhardt had given her an earful on the way out, as well. Thaddeus sat in his comfortable chair for hours, staring at the bundle of laundry. Mrs. Eberhardt brought him a tray with some supper on it before turning in for the night, but it sat untouched on his side table.

At a very late hour, he decided to go to bed. He stood and picked up the bundle and took it to his room. He opened it to let the wrinkles fall out and found a small box at the center. He opened it and found a note as well as a very expensive-looking set of cuff links. He read the note.

"Dearest Thaddeus, I hope it is okay that I call you that. I have enjoyed your company immensely. I pray that you feel the way that I do, that we have developed something more than a simple master/laundress relationship. I may be just a silly Irish girl, but I count the minutes until you show up on my doorstep each morning with your bundle of laundry. You have given me so much over the last few months, not the least of which is my freedom. I wished to give you something in return that is equally precious. You have my love and deep admiration for what it is worth and this small token, as well. If my love be unrequited, please feel no issue towards me. But if it is, let us embrace it. I know we are at very different stations, but I care not. I hope you may say the same. Our meeting may seem an accident of chance but I believe it to be more divinely inspired. Let us remember the words of Shakespeare: 'Love sought is good, but given unsought is better.' Yours Truly, Mary."

Thaddeus dropped the note. He sat down hard on his bed. Mary wanted to buy him something so badly she did the only thing she could think of to pay for it. *That poor, misguided girl,* he thought. He knew that in her own way, this was an expression of love. *I have made a grave mistake,* he thought.

He had to see her. He could explain to her why what she did was wrong and he could forgive her if she could forgive his impertinence. He grabbed his coat and headed for the door. He realized the hour as his hand touched the door and he felt for the revolver in his inner pocket. He hadn't occasion to use it in years, but he felt better knowing it was there.

He moved down the street, almost running. He hailed a Hansom cab and rode the ten blocks to her apartment in a few minutes. It was very late, but this part of the city never fully slept. There was loud music and revelers on the street all night every night. It was well after midnight before he found his way up to her room.

When he got to her door he noticed the light was on. The small, frosted window next to the door had been broken for many weeks and, as usual she had hung her heavy coat over it. He had offered to have it fixed, but she had declined.

He knocked on the door and there was no answer. He knocked louder and still no answer. He announced himself through the door and not a word came back. He reached in through the window and pushed the coat aside. On the bed lay what appeared to be a human form, bloody and mutilated.

Overcome with emotion, Thaddeus screamed, "murder!" The only spiritual gift Hydogall had bestowed on Thaddeus was his strength. Thaddeus had never asked for it, but Hydogall gave it just the same. He kicked the door open and there lay the horribly disfigured remains of Mary Kelly. He knew it was her based on the

148

color of the hair that remained, and destroyed dress lying underneath her. He gagged to avoid vomiting, tears streaking down his face. He felt faint.

A barely audible chuckle came from the small closet across the room. *The murderer is still here,* he thought. He strode quickly to the closet door and flung it open. No one was there. The same chuckle came from underneath the bed, a little louder this time. He quickly moved to the bed and looked underneath. It was dark, but no one was there. He heard the chuckle in the hallway and moved to the door. A man was running towards the stairs very quickly. Too quickly for a normal human being.

"Hydogall, is he one of you?" he said as he gave chase.

"I believe so, Thaddeus. I can the feel the presence of another and it certainly fits what we have just seen. Thaddeus, I am so sorry about Mary."

"We'll mourn Mary later! For now, we must catch this brigand!"

They chased him into the dimly lit alleyway in the back of the building. Hydogall whispered, "I believe I know this individual. Judging by his movement around the room, I believe this to be Dagnem, a former Angel of Death. Keep a close eye on the shadows. He can move between them like holes in space."

"I hate alleys, Old Friend. Bad things happen here."

Thaddeus withdrew his revolver from his coat. He held it close to his body so it could not be knocked from his hand. "Show yourself, coward!" He yelled.

The chuckling came again. In the close confines of the alley, it seemed to come from everywhere. Suddenly, a form lunged at Thaddeus from his left side. The revolver in his right hand was pressed against his abdomen when the attacker grabbed it, pulling his hand and forearm into the shadow. Thaddeus pulled on his hand with all his might, squeezing the trigger on the revolver reflexively. Blood and tissue splattered outward from the shadow as Thaddeus fell backward, stumbling.

He stepped back towards the shadow where there was much blood, but no body. It was then he noticed the revolver in his hand was missing the barrel. It appeared to have been sheared clean off near the base. He quickly took his handkerchief from his pocket and cleaned his hand and face off as he walked out of the alley.

Thaddeus walked the entire ten blocks home, hoping to avoid any police. It was nearly four in the morning when he reached his flat. As an attorney, he had been involved in several murder trials so he knew exactly what to do to avoid evidence and suspicion.

He removed his clothes inspecting each item for blood stains. Finding some on his coat only, he ripped it up and placed it in the freshly stoked fire. He made sure every last scrap was consumed. He washed his shoes by hand, scrubbing them thoroughly. He double checked his remaining clothes, then bundled them up to be disposed of on his morning walk to work. He then bathed, scrubbing his hands and face vigorously.

Though he knew he would get little sleep, he dressed in his night shirt and lay in his bed. "Hydogall?" he asked. "What happened to the murderer?"

"I cannot say for sure, but I believe the body simply ceased to be the moment the bullet entered his brain. The man's mind was controlling his movement through the shadows and once he could not do that, the shadows closed up, sealing off the other side. They will likely find his remains nearby, since he cannot move very far."

"And Dagnem?"

"Back in Hell."

"I will never know what happened, I'm sure. Did Mary invite another man to her quarters? Did he simply come in on his own after she had gone inside?" He shook his head. "I know she was a good woman deep down and I shall miss her deeply." And with that, he whispered a quote from a Shakespearean sonnet she had been so fond of, "hear my soul speak. Of the very instant that I saw you, Did my heart fly at your service." Thaddeus began to weep softly and soon fell asleep from exhaustion.

***

"That is so sad," Patty said.

"Indeed," Hydogall replied. "Thaddeus never got over Mary. He never married or courted anyone. Upon his death some twenty years later, he left all of his substantial estate to various charities after setting up a fund for Mrs. Eberhardt, who would live until the age of ninety-five. He was a good man and I still miss him to this day."

"Did you know it was The Ripper you had killed?" Dylan asked.

"Not for a few days. The Whitechapel murders, as they were called, had been happening on and off for two years. It took a few days for the press to link Mary to The Ripper. There were a few cases after Mary that were similar but executed by other sick persons. Officially, she was the last victim. Sadly, I have no idea who the man really was. They did find a body behind a trash bin further down the alley a few days later, but it was never linked to Mary's murder, since he died from a head wound."

"So, it was dumb luck that you were able to kill him?" Dylan asked.

"Yes, I am afraid so. By all rights, he had the advantage in that darkened alleyway. I am positive that Dagnem was not in control of his Vessel as he is now. He never would have been so…sloppy."

Ten minutes later they were pulling into Melanie's apartment complex. Dylan saw that Melanie's car was already being packed up. "I guess we should say goodbye now. I don't want to clue Melanie in on what's happening."

"Dylan, I'm scared for you." She hugged him tight.

"I'm certainly scared, too, but it has to be this way. I can concentrate on him completely and not worry about you. Well, I'll still worry about you, but you know what I mean."

"Yeah, I get it. I don't like it, but I get it. Do you have a plan?"

"Sort of. I'm gonna stay at Rusty's cabin. Unless his sister has made her way there. If she shows up, well, I'll be hard to see."

"Smart thinking, since Dagnem never met Rusty."

"Yeah. Then I'll patrol at night looking for him. I know what he looks like and I can literally walk down the street without anyone seeing me. If he is still in Laramie, he should show up eventually."

"It may take some time that way. Do you have any leads about where he is staying?"

"Nope, but I'm guessing he won't be far from the train yards since many of his victims were found there. He can't travel through shadows very far."

They got out and walked up to Melanie's ground floor apartment. Melanie opened the door just as they got there. "Hey you!" She was talking to Patty, who was in the lead. They hugged tightly and then she turned to Dylan. "Fessor, always nice to see you." She had called Dylan that name ever since she was a little girl. Dylan had said he wanted to be a professor some day and she couldn't pronounce the whole word. She hugged him even tighter. "How are you guys doin'?"

Dylan looked at Patty. "Better. You know, time heals all wounds."

"For sure," she replied. They went inside and talked a bit, but soon Dylan made the excuse that it was getting late and he needed to drive back. He gave each of them another quick hug, told them not to have too much fun, and he was off.

Chapter 11 – Fight

Dylan and Hydogall spoke a lot about battle tactics on the drive home. They each had some ideas about how to approach Dagnem, but the hardest part would be finding him. When Dylan got back to town, he pulled into his driveway. He took his bags out of the trunk, including his gear, and walked around to the back of the house. He looked around, then became invisible and took to the air. He quickly moved high into the air, since the bags he carried weren't invisible. He flew in the direction of Rusty's cabin and within a few minutes he was there. He hovered above it for a while, making sure no one was around, then descended.

He wasn't sure why the bags didn't turn invisible, and he asked Hydogall.

"They are not an extension of your body unlike your clothes or a weapon you might be carrying. You will be able to make objects invisible one day, but it takes a great deal of practice and concentration."

He checked the door and it was locked. He placed his thumb on the scanner and the door popped open. He took his bags upstairs, hiding them in the closet of the room he had stayed in before. He wasn't sure how long he would be staying and he didn't want anyone that might be showing up when he wasn't around to know he was staying there.

The freezer had quite a bit of frozen food. He warmed up some lasagna and ate greedily. He realized he hadn't had anything to eat since the morning. The sun was going down outside, and he decided to get ready for the evening patrol. As he walked up the stairs to his room, he noticed a short sword on the wall.

"Hydogall, you said any weapon I carried would be invisible?"

"Yes, Dylan."

Dylan took the short sword from the wall, still in its scabbard. "I would imagine you know quite a bit about swords?"

"That particular weapon appears to be a Roman Gladius. The style is that of those manufactured around 3BC to 100 AD. I have no idea of the provenance, so I cannot judge the authenticity. However, it has a very ornate but well-worn hilt. The rubies alone are worth a great deal of money. The inlay on the scabbard is high grade gold. And from what we know of Dr. Carlson, it is likely authentic."

"Wow," Dylan exclaimed. "Two thousand years old." He moved to put the sword back on the wall.

"Dylan, I would reconsider. It may be an antique, but Roman swords were exquisitely crafted. That one likely belonged to a prominent officer. You would be hard pressed to find a sword of higher quality without visiting feudal Japan."

Dylan held the sword out in front of him. He pulled the sword from the scabbard and could almost swear he heard a small *hiss*. He rolled it over and examined it more closely. He ran his finger across the two-sided blade. "It's certainly very sharp."

"I am sure the leather belt it is attached to is new. It looks far more modern than the rest of it."

"It's not very heavy. What do you think it is made out of?"

"Most likely it was forged from steel. That is what most swords were forged from at the time," Hydogall stated.

"Well, I don't really have a choice. Maybe you can give me some pointers later on how to use this thing."

"Absolutely."

Dylan continued up the stairs, sword in hand. He got dressed in his gear and placed the belt holding the sword around his waist. It was a little clunky when he moved so he tied a piece of string to the bottom on the scabbard and round his lower thigh so it would move less. He thought that perhaps it could be modified to sit on his back later.

Finally, he put his helmet on and became invisible. He walked downstairs, almost tripping since he couldn't see his feet, and headed for the door. He opened it slowly, looking for anyone that might be about, then quickly ventured outside, closing the door behind him.

It was dark outside. The moon had not risen yet and there were no outside lights on the two buildings. He began to rise into the air, slowly at first, before picking up speed and heading towards town.

That night, Dylan flew grid patterns back and forth over Laramie for many hours. He could not find any trace of Dagnem. He did, however, prevent another street fight and helped two guys push start their car without them knowing. At nearly five o'clock, he flew back to the cabin and was asleep on his bed thirty minutes later.

Dylan woke in the afternoon and had a large meal. He showered and spent the rest of the afternoon roaming around the house and shop. They spent another hour working on offensive and defensive swordplay. Afterward, Dylan took a short nap.

Dylan awoke shortly before dark to the sound of a car coming up the drive. He moved around the room quickly, making sure everything was put away. Rusty's niece got out of the car and walked up the front porch. She scanned the area before touching the security pad and walking in. Dylan was hovering invisibly ten feet above her. He was glad he had left the lights off before he had fallen asleep on the couch.

The niece, Martha, took out her cell phone and dialed a number. "I'm there now," she stated. "No, it looks clean. No one has been here recently," she observed. She walked around the room and went upstairs. She stopped halfway up. "Wait," she said looking at

156

the wall. "Simon's sword is gone." She looked around the room, a little more slowly this time. "Hold on," she said.

She continued upstairs and went into the rooms, where Dylan couldn't see. He heard dressers and closets being opened and some low talking. She came out and walked straight out the front door, closing it quickly behind her. She was talking more animatedly into the phone on the porch. Then she got into her car and pulled away.

"Great," Dylan lamented. "The one antique that belongs to someone else and I take that one. I thought everything here belonged to Rusty."

"But, Dylan, the sword is in your closet, not hidden. She surely must have seen it."

"Maybe not. I don't know. I feel bad, though."

Dylan quickly heated up some food and ate. Then he dressed and was outside before long. He took to the air, becoming invisible as he did. He flew towards town in the dark night sky.

He smelled the smoke before he saw the flames. There was a large brick building on fire downtown. Dylan couldn't remember which business it housed as he flew towards it, but there were people inside near the windows and on the roof top.

Dylan grabbed two people on the roof without stopping. He nearly knocked the wind out of both of them before depositing them on the roof of the building across the street. The next two were the last ones on the roof and they struggled when he grabbed them around their waists. They had seen the other two be taken before them.

"It's okay, I've got you!" Dylan said loudly.

"What the heck, man!" one of the screamed.

"I'm getting you to safety," he explained.

He dropped them off on the other roof top and one had the presence of mind to yell, "thanks!" in no particular direction. Dylan flew in through one of the top windows. The top level had flames here and there and was filled with smoke.

"I count eight people, Dylan. Three women and five men. Four are unconscious along the south wall. The other four are getting ready to jump from the east window. They will be severely injured by a fall from this height."

"Wait!" Dylan shouted as he ran toward the east window. "Let me help you down!" This time he became visible so they could see him. He went through them and knocked the window out along with some of the surrounding brick making a large opening in the wall. He scooped up the two girls, one in each arm. The two men he told to hold on around his neck and waist. It was awkward, but he moved through the large opening and lowered them all down to the ground.

As soon as all four let go, he rose again and entered the building. He grabbed the first he saw on the ground. "Easy buddy, I've got you."

"My—my friends?" the young man asked.

"Four from the roof rescued. Four rescued from this room so far and you four make twelve. Are there any others left in the building?"

"T—twelve? There's only eleven of us at the party…"

Suddenly Dylan was hit from behind very hard. He flew into the wall and slid down. Something was broken on his left side. Maybe a rib or two. He stumbled to stand only to see Dagnem standing before him. Dagnem thrust his gauntleted hand hard at Dylan's chest. Instead of penetrating deep, it stopped short, breaking several points off completely. He stumbled backward, holding his wrist and hand.

"I should have your heart in my hand!" Dagnem yelled incredulously.

"Kevlar plates, Brainiac. If it stops a bullet, it can stop your pig stickers!" Dylan silently thanked Rusty for the vest. Dylan flew at Dagnem hard and fast knocking him across the room. As he turned to face the three downed people, Dagnem hit him hard from the same side. He had jumped through a shadow on one side of the room and came out the other side.

"You will not save yourself, much less any others, Hydogall!"

Dylan could see a red Ladder Truck outside. The ladder was cranking up towards the large hole he had made. He had to get Dagnem out of there so the fire firefighters could do their job. He became invisible. As he hoped, the smoke swirled as he moved but there was too much to be able to pinpoint him as long as he kept moving.

"Show yourself, coward!" Dagnem screamed, mouth foaming as he yelled.

"A coward uses innocent lives for their own gain!" Hydogall yelled in reply.

"Let's step outside, jerk!" Dylan said as he swooped in and grabbed Dagnem around the waist. He flew fast out of the large hole in the wall, narrowly missing the top of the ladder as it hit its mark. The fire fighters were already running up to get the survivors.

Dylan took Dagnem high into the air as those on the ground watched in amazement. Dagnem was clawing at Dylan's back, ripping his leather jacket to shreds. Finally, Dagnem found a part of his back that wasn't covered in Kevlar. Dylan screamed.

"There's no shadows up here, Dagnem. If I drop you, you die!" Dylan said.

"These naked monkeys are so narrow minded, Hydogall!" Dagnem screamed. He jabbed two claws hard into Dylan's side. Dylan yelled and let go of Dagnem. He fell nearly a hundred feet, disappearing into a dark alley.

Dylan was bleeding profusely from his left side, the same side with broken ribs. He scanned the area and saw the firefighters retreating down their ladder with the remaining injured people. He landed near the firefighter he assumed to be in charge. Dylan could see his helmet had the word 'Chief' on it.

"Holy—" the man yelled when he landed.

"It's okay, Sir, Chief. I'm here to help." Dylan raised his visor, confident his identity was safe, especially in the low light conditions. "Do we know if everyone is out?" The Chief just stared at Dylan with wide eyes.

"There is no time to explain!" He yelled. "I'm fireproof. If there is anyone still inside I can get them out."

"No, no," the Chief replied. "They told us there were only eleven people in the building. They were having some kind of party when the fire broke out in the lower floor. Some man came in and started fighting with them, wouldn't let them leave." He looked down at Dylan's wound. "Son, let my guys patch you up. You're going to bleed out."

"I have to go. He's getting away."

"Wait just a second," the Chief exclaimed. "He turned around and grabbed a small bag. "We keep this emergency bag in the cab in case of gunshot wounds." He opened the bag and took out a tampon and a small bottle of alcohol. "This is going to hurt," he said squeezing the alcohol bottle into the wounds. Dylan screamed behind clenched teeth. Before he stopped, the Chief jammed half a tampon in each hole in his side. The bleeding stopped immediately. "That's a band aid young man. Get some real help as soon as you can. Now go!"

Dylan took to the air saying, "Thanks! Keep everyone out of the alley," as he moved toward the alley. He landed at its opening and walked into the darkness. Remembering the sword, he took it from its scabbard and held it up as Hydogall had instructed him. "Dagnem! Show yourself!" Dylan yelled, the act itself sending white hot bolts of pain down his side.

The low laughter started above him, then it was beside him, then behind. "I am everywhere, Hydogall. You know that." Next came a high-pitched screech that increased in volume and seemed to come from everywhere. Suddenly, Dagnem lunged from his left side. Dylan spun the sword around and barely deflected his strike.

"You have taught him a few things, Hydogall," Dagnem marveled after disappearing back into the shadows. Dylan looked up just as Dagnem pounced from above. He didn't get the sword up in time and the sharp claws of the gauntlet racked across the top of his helmet, snapping his neck backward quickly. Dylan fell on his back as Dagnem hit him hard on the side of the helmet. It was a wild swing and lacked his full strength. Still, it spun Dylan sideways. He slid on his back and came up four feet in the air. He kicked Dagnem hard in the shoulder. His arm went limp from dislocation.

Dagnem screamed in pain. His gauntleted hand clutched at his shoulder. He dove into the shadows and emerged on the roof where Dylan saw him looking down from the corner of his eye. He flew up to the roof as Dagnem leapt into another shadow, coming out onto another rooftop.

Dylan chased Dagnem from rooftop, to alleyway, to rooftop for long minutes. Obviously starting to panic, Dagnem stopped for a moment to look around. As he did, he purposely banged his shoulder into a brick chimney. He screamed and grabbed his shoulder but then

161

rolled it around, showing it was back in use. Then he dove into a shadow and was lost.

Dylan rose into the air, looking at all of the rooftops in the area. "He has to be close," he murmured. "He has to see where he is going." Then it caught his eye. The tallest building in the area was the Astronomy building at the college five blocks east. He could see dim lights on the roof from his vantage.

Dylan flew as fast as he could towards the building. He overshot it, doing an impromptu flyover. He saw Dagnem, who hadn't seen Dylan approach, hiding in a corner. He flew up behind him slowly, then stepped up his speed at the last minute. Dagnem's spun around, hitting Dylan across the top of his helmet with a heavy, metal pipe just as he reached him. The helmet shattered, sending shards of plastic and foam in every direction. Dylan blacked out.

When he awoke, his hands were bound in front of him. There was blood running down his face, clouding his vision. Dagnem was standing in front of him, pacing back and forth. His shredded jacket and vest were lying next to him.

"Oh, good, it is not dead. Since you were not speaking, Hydogall, I thought maybe its brain was damaged beyond repair."

Hydogall replied, "I do not respond when my Vessel is incapacitated!"

"Ever the servant, eh Brother? Oh, do not bother to struggle. I used the straps from your vest to bind you. While they were rather easy to rip from the vest, they are nigh unbreakable even by your strong hands."

Dylan pulled and pulled with no reward.

"He is a slow learner, is he not Brother? Next time try indwelling someone a little smarter. Take mine, for example. Say hello again, Sven."

"Hello again, Sven," came a different voice from Dagnem's lips.

"Ha! Sven was a lowly insurance adjuster, but a true genius where it matters. He had been killing women for many years right under the noses of the local constabulary. His story was an old one, I am afraid. Father did not love him enough, Mother loved him too much. Former lover posted pictures of his stunted manhood on the internet. Former lover ends up in small pieces strewn along five-hundred miles of interstate. You know, that old story. Yet, his bloodlust was unsated. He had killed dozens of women before I ever found him. Together we have killed nearly a hundred, including your diminutive older friend the other day." He turned to look at Dylan. "I am sorry about that, but he should not have been involved in this. His sins were minimal, but as they say, you cannot make an omelet without breaking a few old Hebrews."

"Is that what you did with Mary?" Dylan asked, obviously trying to buy some time.

"Who?"

"Mary Kelly!" Hydogall screamed. "The woman you killed before Thaddeus Cray returned the favor!"

"If only he could have killed me. Death would have been preferable to Hell," Dagnem stated, anger building. He shook his head as he paced. "I remember this wench. Her sins were many. I saw her earlier in the day and waited for her to return home. I propositioned her, but she seemed distraught and no amount of money would sway her. So, I waited for her to lie down, then sprang on top of her from the shadows as I have done a thousand times. A thousand times a thousand actually. She barely resisted as I cut her throat. She had already resolved to die, I think. It was really…anti-climactic, but her heart….her heart was a feast to remember."

"You…sick…freak," Dylan intoned slowly. He was talking to Dagnem, but looking at his sword, which lay five feet in front of him. He had to keep Dagnem talking while he worked out his plan. If he could get to the sword quickly and quietly without Dagnem seeing him, he had a chance.

"What's your endgame here, Dagnem? How does this end?" Dylan asked.

Dagnem was still pacing. "I could just kill your Vessel and be done with it. Although that is not very poetic. You are not a simple murder, Hydogall. I have dreamed of this moment for over a century. A drop in the well for those such as you and I, but a century in Hell lasts a thousand lifetimes. I could remove your heart and let your last sight be me devouring it. Your Vessels sins are numerous and as I said before, he is not protected. His heart would be very tasty. You could visit with him in Hell."

Dagnem rubbed his chin as he looked out over Laramie. "Or, now picture this, I could find the Vessels mate and kill her in front of you, then let you spend a few days staring at her lifeless body. Oh, the intense sorrow would tenderize the heart muscle better than any vinegar preparation could do." Dagnem shook his head in the affirmative. "That is it. That is what I will do."

Dagnem spun around and stood before Dylan, his hands still bound, with the sword in his hands in a classic 'batter-up' stance. Dagnem's eyes grew wide as Dylan swung and connected with his lower abdomen, leaving a two-inch-deep gouge across it.

Dagnem stumbled back.

"Make sure your next Vessel watches more TV. The bad guy always loses when he monologues." Dylan struck again, running the blade through Dagnem's right side.

"Your time here is over, Brother. Time to go back to Hell," Hydogall said.

Dagnem was bleeding profusely as he stumbled back off the blade. His injuries were grave, but survivable. He was quickly looking from side to side as Dylan advanced on him. There was a shadow to his right and he lunged toward it. Dylan swung, but missed, as Dagnem appeared to use his last burst of speed. Just as he reached the shadow and entered head first, a bright light shined on him.

"What's going on up here?" Yelled a voice from the stairway door. Dylan looked over to see Neville holding a bright flashlight. He spun back around to where Dagnem had entered the shadow and beheld a gruesome sight. Dagnem's head and torso had been inside the shadow when the light hit it, but not his lower half. That part remained on the roof.

Dylan walked slowly over to the remains just to make sure what he saw was real. It was. Neville shined the light in Dylan's face and he turned away. His helmet was gone, but his face was covered in blood. He hoped it would be enough to keep Neville from recognizing him.

"What the heck was that?!" Neville asked.

"Evil. Pure evil," Dylan replied, making his voice somewhat deeper. "Call the police. Tell them that this man is the serial killer they're looking for. The rest of his body will be somewhere close by. Near a shadow. His name is Sven."

"And who are you, Sir?" Neville asked.

Dylan thought about it and replied, "Call me Hyde." With those words, he swooped over, grabbing his jacket and vest and flew off into the night.

Chapter 12 - After

Laramie, WY became a media firestorm for the next week. Some news outlets had already sent some junior-level staff to report on the serial murders, but had called in the big guns when the murderer was taken out by a mysterious flying man. Neville had been interviewed by every major network including cable and foreign press. They were calling the hero 'Hyde' much to Dylan's delight.

Patty had spoken to Dylan the same night of the battle. Not wanting to arouse suspicion from Melanie, they continued their week-long trip as if nothing had happened. She called Dylan often over the remaining days, though.

Dylan was covered in cuts and bruises and knew he likely had a concussion. Not to mention, two large puncture wounds in his side. He had gone home to change, then drove to the emergency room. The staff believed he had been downtown when the fire broke out and was hit by debris. Sadly, there were others there suffering from similar injuries. Luckily, most were minor. He stayed there overnight and was released early the next day with stitches in his side and head.

Since he was still on leave from work, he didn't need to return to campus. The few times he had ventured out during the week, the name, 'Hyde' was still on everyone's lips. This made Dylan happy.

By the following Saturday, the town had settled down. Much of the media had departed for more recent news. Dylan would be leaving to pick up Patty later in the day. He was sitting on his front porch enjoying an iced tea, when a white van pulled up in front of his home. Rusty's niece, Martha, stepped out of the driver side. She had a frozen coffee drink in one hand and a large manila envelope in the other.

Dylan stood as she approached. She waved as she walked up the stairs. "It's good to see you again, Dylan," she smiled, taking his outstretched hand.

"You, too, Martha. I thought you would have been gone by now. Please have a seat." He motioned to the other chair.

"Thanks," she said, sitting down. "I am actually on my way to the airport, but I needed to stop by here first. All the paperwork has been done and the Will has been finalized. I tried to reach you earlier in the week so you could meet with the lawyer."

"I had a slight accident," Dylan explained, pointing to the small bandage on his forehead.

"I see that. Looks nasty," she observed, staring at the bandage. "What happened?"

"Wrong place at the wrong time. I was downtown when that building caught fire and that serial killer got killed. Some debris fell off the building and hit me. It looks worse than it is."

"I heard about that. Some big fight between two…what…people?"

"They were definitely people, but not normal."

"Wow, right here in little ol' Laramie, eh?" She handed him the envelope. "This is no big, you can meet with the lawyer later to sign the papers."

"Papers?" Dylan asked.

"Yeah. Apparently, my uncle really liked you. He left you his cabin."

"What?" Dylan's eyes were wide.

"Yeah, and everything in it. All you need to do is sign the papers. Oh, and his estate will pay any transfer fees and taxes, as well. He was loaded."

"I can't accept that. It's too much…" Dylan stammered.

"If you don't, it will mean a lot of paperwork for me. I'm his only living relative and I don't want it. I already have more money than I can spend." She looked at him with a serious look on her face. "Please don't make another headache for me." She handed him the envelope which contained a list of assets including the cabin and all the catalogued items within. A picture of Rusty's house in Laramie was in the folder, too.

"He left me his house, too?"

"No. That was left to Patty, but I haven't been able to get hold of her. I was hoping you would let her know. It's a lovely place. He always said a family should live there. Just a 'heads up', though, most of the antiques and such have been removed. He donated them to a museum in Israel. I'm taking them there along with his body. And between you and me, it's not my favorite place to visit. Too much history."

"I don't know what to say," Dylan said in bewilderment.

"Don't say anything. My uncle is, was, an incredible judge of character. I'm sure you'll both do right by him."

"You're sure about all of this? I wouldn't feel right if you wanted it. You were his family."

"From what he told me about you two, you are as much family as I am."

"I just can't believe he did this."

"Believe it." With that, Martha moved in for a hug. Dylan reciprocated. "Thank you for being such a good friend to Rusty. Tell Patty I'm sorry I missed her." She waved as she walked to her car.

"I will," Dylan replied. He waved back and watched as she got into her car. He continued to wave as she pulled away.

Martha looked in the rearview mirror at the figure in the low light of the rear storage area. "You should have just got out with me. You could have gotten one more good look at him without the tinted window between you. I doubt he would have recognized you."

"No, that chapter is closed. It's best not to tempt fate, my friend," came the reply.

***

Dylan stared at the paperwork for several minutes. He walked into his house and closed the door. He came out the back door invisible and took to the sky. He flew to Rusty's cabin, *his* cabin, a few minutes later. Applying his thumb to the lock, the door popped open.

Inside, the cabin looked the same. All of the furnishings and knickknacks appeared undisturbed. However, there was a new picture on the wall. It might have been there before, but Dylan didn't think he would have missed it. The painting was of a young man, dressed in typical pioneer garb, panning for gold. He stared at it closely and realized it bore a strong resemblance to Rusty. Dylan shook his head, laughing.

He sat down on the couch and looked around the room. "Thanks, Rusty," he said aloud. Then he noticed the shiny silver tray on the table. He wasn't sure how it got there, but he picked it up and stared at it. The image was of himself, only different like before. He smiled big and the reflection smiled back, only not as big.

He stood back up and walked towards the door. He needed to leave to pick up Patty soon. As he got to the door, Hydogall interrupted him.

"Dylan, I have something to tell you."

"What is it, buddy?"

"I am leaving," Hydogall said.

"Leaving?" Dylan asked. "How? Why?"

"It is time. I told you what happened to other Vessels when their spouses found out about me. I do not want that to happen to you and Patty."

"You can't go back to Hell! Patty wouldn't want that."

"I am sure she would not, but that is my decision."

Dylan walked back over to the silver tray. "It seems crazy to go through all of this and then lose you. You're my friend. More than that, you're part of me. I need your guidance."

"You did fine without me for most of your life, Dylan. We will miss each other, but it needs to be this way. It is well with me. Let it be well with you also."

Dylan was silent. He stared at the reflection through tears. Finally, he asked, "Will you stay long enough for Patty to say goodbye?"

"No, it is best if I go now. I do not wish to see her sadness," Hydogall said.

"I can't believe you are going," Dylan lamented, a hitch in his voice.

"I have been honored to share your life, Dylan. Your father would be so proud of the man you have become."

Dylan was crying now. "Thank you for everything, Hydogall."

"You are welcome, Dylan. Before I go you should know something about your abilities."

"Of yeah, I guess I need to call a cab." Dylan wiped his eyes.

"No, you do not. The reason The Fallen don't often share their spiritual gifts with their Vessels is because once they are shared, they cannot be taken back."

"But, they are your gifts?" Dylan questioned.

170

"Correct, and mine to bestow as I see fit. Spiritual gifts cannot be taken back save by the Almighty Himself. They are a part of you now."

"So, you will still have them?"

"As I said, only the Father may take them back."

"Thank you again, my friend," Dylan said, his voice still trembling. He stared at the reflection that was mostly like his when suddenly it changed to being exactly his. Dylan was silent for a moment, then gently asked, "Hydogall?" There was no reply.

Dylan's drive to Fort Collins felt very long. He thought about what Hydogall must be going through. The torment he was so afraid of. Dylan shuddered as he thought of it.

Patty was very happy to see him. Their embrace was very long and silent. Melanie excused herself several minutes into it after noticing Patty and Dylan were both crying bit. She had no idea what they had been through, other than the death of their friend, and chalked it up to pent up emotion.

On the drive home, Dylan told Patty about Hydogall's departure. She was, as expected, very sad. At the same time, there was some relief that she was finally, truly alone with Dylan.

"So, how do you know he's really gone?" she asked. "Maybe he's faking it just to make me feel better."

"No," Dylan replied, "I can tell. I can feel something missing. I can't explain it completely, but I'm sure he's gone."

Patty was thoughtful for a minute then she spoke. "Turn here," she said, pointing to the upcoming intersection.

"Why? That's not the way to Laramie."

"Well, you need a new helmet."

***

Melanie was running late for her night shift. The week she had off with Patty was fun, but she would be paying for it in traded shifts. She parked her car near the side entrance of the hospital even though it was dimly lit. When she came out in the morning, she wanted to walk as little as possible to get to her car.

As she got out, she noticed two men approaching. She thought nothing of it as there were often people milling around outside.

"Hi, ma'am," the taller one began. "You have some change I could have? Our car is out of gas and we need to get to Oklahoma by morning."

"Oh, I'm sorry," Melanie replied. "I don't usually carry cash." She felt a little uneasy now.

"That's okay," he replied. "We take credit cards." The smaller one lunged at Melanie, grabbing her purse. Melanie, ever the feisty one, resisted. He tugged harder and she came towards him, not letting go of her purse. He grabbed her around the neck and the taller one produced a knife.

"Well, maybe we'll just take you with us, too," he said. "I promise we'll all have a good time." The shorter one began dragging her towards an old van. Melanie struggled and then her vision began to blur...

Epilogue #1 – Rusty's Story

The Morning After Rusty's Death

Mara got the call at two in the morning. She had been sound asleep in her bed, *or* hotel room and the ringing phone startled her. Calls in the middle of the night were never a good sign in her experience.

"Hello?" she asked as she answered.

"Hi, Mara, it's Tabitha. We need you in Laramie."

Mara shook the fog out of her head. "He's dead?"

"Yeah. They called me as his next of kin but I'm in the middle of the California thing. Can you get away?"

"Yeah, it's pretty quiet right now. I'll call the airport and get the jet fueled."

"Awesome. I'm emailing you everything we have. Your name is Martha and you're his niece."

Mara laughed. "Really, he named his niece after his sister?"

"I know, right? I guess at our age using names that mean something to you is just easier to remember."

Mara checked her tablet. "Looks like the file came through. I should be in Laramie by morning."

"Perfect, that's what I told them," Tabitha replied.

Mara called the airport and had them begin fueling her jet and prepping for takeoff. It was a small airport, but they did have basic services like these for pilots. Her jet was a small one, so it shouldn't take long. Within two hours, she was in the air.

The flight wouldn't be long. She set the autopilot and took out the tablet. Luckily, he was an incredible note taker and, unlike Mara, updated his notes each night. He wrote about Dylan and Patty.

173

He wrote about the discovery of Hydogall. He wrote about the Fallen Dagnem. His last entry was just last night. *Probably right before it happened,* she thought. She finished the file just as she was approaching the airport in Laramie.

Mara landed and made the arrangements for fuel and maintenance. She expected to be back by week's end. The clerk at the car rental desk told her of a nice new hotel near the University and she was able to check in before noon. It was something that she had done many times before.

The mortuary was extremely helpful. Per his Living Will, his body was to be left unprepared. The remains were to be placed into a coffin he had already chosen and sealed. It would then be taken to Israel and placed in his family mausoleum. The body had been cleaned and sealed in the coffin by the time she arrived.

"The college set up a memorial for tomorrow. Will you be able to attend or do you need to leave ASAP?" the mortician asked in the polite tone they all seem to speak in.

"I'll stick around, but I'll need to transport the body now. I want to get it loaded into my jet before he starts to smell." Mara chuckled a little. The mortician gave an uneasy, forced laugh.

"You may store the remains here if you like. We have a cold room. It will help."

"Thank you for the offer, but it's okay. The cargo hold is completely sealed and I'm sure you did an excellent job sealing the coffin, as well. It's a silly tradition, but our family doesn't like to let the body out of our sight for too long. You know, we Jews have some odd traditions." She felt funny pulling her 'Hebrew Card', especially since she wasn't Jewish, well, not in some time anyway, but the fib usually worked with the Gentiles.

She drove to Rusty's house in Laramie. She got out to open the garage door and backed the van in. She shut the large door and secured it from the inside. She went into the house and searched the entire premises for occupants. She shut all of the blinds and drapes and bolted the two entry doors. She then made four peanut butter and jelly sandwiches and two tall glasses of goat's milk, which she left on the kitchen table. On her way back to the garage, she grabbed a throw blanket.

She opened the back door to the van and stepped inside. Using a crowbar, she pried the coffin lid back and forth until it broke free. She lifted it all of the way open.

Inside was the naked body of a man who looked to be nearly thirty. His body had not a single scar. His beard was thick, but short and his hair was shoulder length.

"Rise, Lazarus!" she cried.

Rusty opened his eyes. "That never gets old for you, does it?"

"Nope never," she said throwing the blanket over him.

"I wish you would cover me before I wake. For crying out loud, girl, your father was a priest!"

"Yeah, but Jairus quit working in the synagogue after I was brought back. Started following the Disciples around like they were the Grateful Dead. Technically I was a preacher's daughter after that and you know what they say about us." She laughed.

"Still, I could be your father. It's obscene." Rusty started crawling out of the van as he spoke, the blanket wrapped around him.

"Come on, Lazarus, we're both nearly two millennia old. When are you going to start treating me like an adult?"

"When I don't have to see a twelve-year-old girl every time you come back." They walked into the house, Rusty spying the sandwiches and milk on the table. "But you are indeed an incredible woman," he praised, hurrying over to the table and grabbing a sandwich. "I'm starving," he mumbled, through a full mouth.

They sat and ate and talked for hours. They reminisced about the many times each had picked up each other's remains. They spoke of their many shared acquaintances. Most of all, they discussed what was currently going on in Laramie.

"Dagnem is very dangerous," Rusty said. "I worry about Dylan and Patty. I pray they are strong enough to face him."

"Seems capable from the file," Mara replied

"He is very capable and has a wonderful partner in Patty, but I can't help but worry. Rusty continued eating then asked, "how were you able to retrieve my body so quickly? With the FBI investigation, I would think they would have had to hold onto my remains a little longer."

"You know we have friends in the FBI. They put pressure on their local agents to get all the pictures and tissue samples and such done early this morning. 'Officially' it was for religious purposes. In reality, there has been no shortage of bodies from this investigation and none have provided any forensic evidence other than the hole in the heart and the occasional missing limbs. Your body was the least mutilated so there was nothing really valuable in terms of the investigation."

"Well," Rusty replied, "I've never been so happy to have little value." Both chuckled as they continued eating.

The next day, Mara dressed for the memorial. "Are you coming," she asked.

"Yes, but I'll just walk. If we are seen together, there might be suspicion."

***

176

At the memorial, Rusty was moved to tears more than once by the speakers. He watched Dylan and Patty from afar, feeling their pain, wanting desperately to console them. When it was over, he walked home, savoring the beautiful, tree-lined streets. He knew it would be the last time for a long while, but he would be back some day. Like few other places in the world, Laramie, Wyoming was a truly enjoyable place to live. When he returned home, he found Mara already there.

"You really made an impression here, Lazarus."

"I certainly made many friends,"

"You always do."

"What good is this long life unless you truly embrace the living?"

"Is that a dig, Lazarus? Come on, I've had thousands of friends. Buried dozens of husbands. I'm just burnt out on relationships. You know how it is. Every three or four hundred years or so you just have to step back from society. From short-lived relationships. I just prefer to work directly for the group right now." She paused for a moment. "Speaking of the group, I don't know how plugged in you have been lately, but there is something weird going on. Something unlike anything we have seen."

"How do you mean?"

"We've identified nearly a dozen instances of people with superhuman abilities around the world. Most of them are in the United States. Get this, though, none have been identified as Vessels. Other than your boy here in Laramie."

"What? How is that possible? Has their DNA been tested?"

"Many of them have been tested, yeah. They possess specific fragments of angelic DNA, but not the chromosomes necessary to qualify as Vessels. I've personally tested several of them for the presence of the Fallen to no avail. Frankly, we are stumped."

Rusty was astounded. He had never encountered someone with spiritual gifts without being indwelled by the Fallen. It made no sense. Still, Mara was not given to flights of fancy.

"I should have all of your affairs settled in the next week. I've got a crew coming in to pack up the basement tomorrow. Have you thought about where we should ship it? Where are you going to get set up next?"

"Well, if what you are telling me is true, I think I had better spend some time with the group. Tell me, where are the Sons of Aaron calling home these days?"

Epilogue #2 – Neville's Story

The Day After Rusty's Death

He preferred to play it low key these days. Sure, he had dabbled in world domination from time to time, but he had his fill for now. There was no shortage of humans offering themselves up to be Vessels for him specifically, but none really appealed to him. So, when he came across the young Marine with no brain activity lying in a hospital bed in Afghanistan, who also happened to be a Vessel, he knew exactly what to do.

He took control and resumed the young soldier's quiet life in Wyoming. His lack of knowledge of the soldier's family or the town he grew up in was easily covered by his brain injury. It was nice for him to just relax and live a low-key life for a few decades or so.

You can imagine his anger when a silly little former Angel of Death decided to start a multi-state killing spree that ended up in his sleepy little town. He knew from the news descriptions of the body mutilations that it had Dagnem written all over it.

He had identified Dylan as a Vessel when he first arrived and had been monitoring him for signs of an indwelling. No one ever notices the brain damaged janitor in the background. Every time that stupid bus picked him up and dropped him off at home, he would make his way back to campus to spy on Dylan and his friends. Though Rusty had never realized it, they had met several times over the millennia, when he was indwelling other Vessels.

He had listening devices in Dylan's office and home as well as Rusty's home. He hadn't bothered to bug Patty's place because Dylan didn't spend much time there. He wasn't surprised when he heard Rusty and Patty speaking with Hydogall a couple of weeks ago. He was relieved to find out it was Hydogall, a former Watcher. They were a quiet bunch, but they were formidable. He was hopeful they could dispatch Dagnem before he had to step in.

When Dagnem came into the building looking for Hydogall's Vessel, he was glad he had insured the building was always cold. It was a simple matter each night to reset the computer controlled thermostats located in the basement. He had originally done this to throw off Rusty and Hydogall when he first started working in the building, but it worked against Dagnem just the same. The brain damage ensured Dagnem would see no sins in the soldier's eyes either.

When Rusty was killed, he was concerned it was over. He began sharpening his knives and seeking out Dagnem during the day. He would give Hydogall a few days to end this, but he was ready to take charge, if needed. He didn't want to expose his Vessel to danger and have to move on, but there were rules and Dagnem was breaking them. If people had evidence demons were real, that meant angels were real, too. That would bring the Father even more followers and he could not abide that. And he certainly wasn't going to let the Father think he couldn't control 'his followers.'

The night it all ended, he was making his rounds around the building as usual. He easily cleaned the entire building within the first few hours of his shift and spent the rest of the evening in other pursuits. He spent hours on the internet every night, causing mischief where he could. Nothing major, but enough to cause a few problems here and there and make him laugh.

He heard the ruckus up on the top of the building and decided to investigate. He slowly opened the door and saw Dagnem monologuing to Dylan. When will people learn to stop talking and just end it? He saw Dylan defeat Dagnem and move in for the killing stroke. As Dagnem jumped for the shadow to escape, he knew exactly what to do. He waited until Dagnem was halfway into the shadow before he shouted and shined the beam of light on him, effectively cutting his body in twine.

He called the police as instructed and just as Dylan had said, the rest of the body was found on the rooftop of the History building not far away. He spent hours recounting what he knew before being released to go home.

Unfortunately, the next week was spent in the limelight he had very much wished to shun. Network television and radio stations hounded him day and night for interviews. He tried to make his disability seem worse so people might not bother him so much, but it didn't work. He knew it wouldn't, considering how well he knew the black heart of Man, but he tried anyway. After two weeks, the fervor died down, and everyone forgot about Neville, the brain-damaged janitor.

Dylan, feeling better, finally visited his office building for a full day's work. He had popped in here and there, but classes were over and he used the time to continue healing. He hoped to see Neville and luckily arrived just as Neville was readying to leave.

"Anything to report, Corporal?" Dylan asked in his best authoritarian voice.

Neville pulled off his ever-present headphones and snapped to attention, responding, "Perimeter is tight, all floors are secure, Sir!"

"I haven't seen you in a while. I understand there was some trouble a few weeks back?"

"Yessir, but it was handled."

"Handled? In what way?" Dylan quizzed him. He wanted to know just what Neville was aware of. Most of his interviews were yes or no questions, his discomfort on camera obvious.

"That hero, Sir. He said his name was Hyde. He took out the bad guy. I don't remember his name."

"His name was Sven, I believe. I understand you played a part, too?"

"I don't think so, Sir. I just pointed my flashlight. I don't carry an M-4 or even a Kabar anymore. The government won't let me."

"I have a feeling you did a lot more than you think, Neville. I don't remember if I ever thanked you for your service to our country, but thank you for that and for what you did in the roof. You're still serving and protecting, Corporal."

"That's the police, Sir. Marines are Always Faithful."

"Yes, you are." Dylan shook his hand and walked up to his office.

***

As he opened the door, the lights were already on. Dylan found that quite odd but figured it was a fluke. He put his things a way and sat at his desk.

"Whoops!" He cried, standing back up quickly. On his chair was his burner cell phone. It was smashed and melted somewhat. He knew he had lost it in the fight, probably in the fire judging by its state. Since he had kept it clean of fingerprints, he wasn't worried about someone finding it and connecting him to it. But someone obviously did. Dylan just stared at phone for long minutes, wondering how it got there.

***

Outside, Neville was getting on his bus. He saluted the driver, who returned it. He sat down on the bench, smiling up at the office window he knew belonged to Dylan. He slid the headphones back over his ears and was glad to hear his favorite song playing. In fact, it was the only one on his playlist.

"Pleased to meet you…don't forget my name…"

Inferno – An Abel Hodges Story

Abel had been sleeping in his small cabin in the middle of the Sierras when the first thunderclap woke him. He knew lightning would be coming soon. Even though it was early in the morning, or late at night, depending on who you asked, he put his jeans on and headed out the door. He knew of a great vantage point to keep an eye out for lightning strikes.

He ran swiftly through the forest floor, then bounded up the side of a tall cliff. A few more leaps and he was on top of the tallest tree for miles. He watched as the lightning lit up the area on the eastern side of the mountain range. After half an hour, he spotted what he most feared; smoke.

The smoke was nearly ten miles from his perch. The many months he had spent living in these woods made it a lot easier to navigate, even in the dark. He used the tops of the trees as much as possible when traveling fast and it usually paid off. Sure enough, fifteen minutes later, he arrived at his destination.

At first glance, all he saw was thick, choking smoke. Soon he found three trees completely engulfed up to their crowns. He quickly ran to the first tree and smashed his fist into its base. Though it was a large tree, at least six feet across, it shuddered and fell over. Splinters shot out everywhere. He did the same to the other two trees, trying his best to make them fall in the same general area.

He focused his attention on the tree that was burning the most. It was easy to see through the smoke and darkness because of the bright flames. The drought had turned this area into a tinderbox. He rolled the massive tree back and forth until it no longer showed flames. He did the same to the other two trees. Then he used his feet to kick large amounts of dirt onto the scorched parts to make sure they were not going to burn again.

Looking around, he found no other flames. He ran around the area to be sure since there was a lot of smoke, and a smoldering fire might not be visible. The sound of truck engines could be heard in the distance.

Abel didn't realize he was so close to a fire road. The hotshot crew got there that fast, which impressed him. Returning to the thick trees, he shimmied up to the top of a tall pine and watched.

The twenty-man crew quickly got out of their trucks and descended into the small valley. They could see the smoke and fanned out in groups to find the ignition source. Abel watched as they found what he had done and saw them actually scratching their heads. Their lighted helmets made it easy to keep track of them and the flash of the lightning, now in the distance, would light up the ground every so often.

A long succession of lightning flashes allowed Abel to see something large approaching one of the five-man groups. He moved in closer and saw a large Black Bear moving swiftly towards the crew. The men obviously didn't hear its approach over their own noise. The bear slowed down as it got closer, stalking the crew.

The group moved back to a small clearing where the other groups were re-assembling. The bear followed slowly on the fringes of the thick tree-line. Abel moved from tree to tree as quietly as he could. While he didn't like to advertise his existence, sometimes it was inevitable. If that bear attacked, he thought, he was going to have to act fast.

As if on cue, the bear lunged out of the woods towards the group. The bear was no more than twenty feet from its primary target when Abel landed in front of its prey, reared back his fist, and punched the bear square on its nose as it tried to barrel over him.

186

The strike carried such force that the bear careened off to the side, falling over in a heap.

Abel walked over to it and lay his ear against its chest. It was, thankfully, still alive. He examined its maw for damage, finding only superficial issues. The bear would be fine in a few hours but sore for days. He picked up the five-hundred-pound bear on his shoulders and turned for the tree-line.

"You're him aren't you?" Someone said behind him. He turned to look at them. All twenty crew members had their eyes trained on him. "The Angel. That's what they call you."

"That's what they call me," Abel replied, bounding off into the darkness. Several cell phones cameras flashed as he moved off. He ran and jumped through five miles of brush and trees before stopping to lay the bear on the ground. He was right next to a stream, so the bear could drink when he woke. He made a mental not to stop back by later and check on him. There were so few bears left in these woods, he sincerely hoped this one would be okay.

***

Several days later, Abel was sitting at a diner in Springville. He usually came into town every two weeks for worship services using good clothes he kept stashed away at his cabin. Afterward, he would go to lunch and socialize a bit with the staff as he read the local paper. He had his tablet that he used nearly every night to keep up with events in the world, but the local paper wasn't online.

As he sat and sipped his coffee, he read an article about a siting of 'The Angel' who saved a group of firefighters from an angry bear. He was surprised how well the article was written, the facts being pretty on point. All twenty crew members were on record, but that was about it. He guessed people weren't all that surprised by the siting's anymore.

A young woman sat down next to him at the counter. She had a large leather portfolio sitting in the chair next to her. She ordered the lunch special and introduced herself to Abel.

"My name is Tabitha," she said, sticking her hand out.

Abel smiled warmly and shook her hand. "I'm Rex," he replied. Abel had taken the name 'Rex' since Abel Hodges was supposed to be dead. Rex had been the name of his childhood friend.

They chatted back and forth for several minutes. Tabitha was an artist currently on the road finding things to stir her artistic passions. 'Rex' explained he was a trapper who preferred to live in the wild most of the time.

Tabitha asked if he would like to see some off her work and he replied that he would love to. She showed him standard pencil sketches of trees and squirrels. He told her they were 'good' and he really meant it. The last page was different. The drawing was of a large circle. Inside it was a hodgepodge of triangles and squares that almost looked like writing.

"That one is different," he observed out loud.

She stared at his face. "Yeah," she replied. "I like to doodle sometimes. Some of my best work started out as doodles." She continued to stare at him.

He shook his head as he looked at it. "Well, I don't know much about art, but I like it." He smiled, closing the portfolio and handing it back to her.

She smiled. "Surprising," she whispered.

"What's that?" he asked.

Tabitha fumbled. "Surprising…that you would like it. It's just doodling."

"I don't know. I guess I'm a color-outside-the-lines kind of guy." Abel finished his lunch as Tabitha finally received hers.

"Well, I had best be off. It was nice talking with you, Tabitha."

"You too, Rex. Be careful in those mountains. I hear the wildlife is getting restless."

As Abel walked to the door, he paid the cashier. Being a gentleman, he paid for Tabitha's meal, as well. Then he walked out the door and up the road, disappearing into a thick stand of trees as he headed to his cabin deep in the woods.

***

Tabitha finished her lunch and asked for the check. The waitress told her that the man she was sitting with had already paid it. She smiled and picked up her portfolio. She walked outside and placed it in the back seat of her car and sat in the driver's seat. She took out her tablet and began making notes.

> The Angel, Kern County, CA
>
> Verified that Abel Hodges is alive and living in the Sierras.
>
> Most likely he is 'The Angel' that the locals keep reporting.
>
> He is sporting a long beard and mustache, but the eyes reveal him.
>
> Obtained a DNA sample from his leftover lunch.
>
> Abel periodically attends church services in Springville and has lunch at a nearby diner afterwards.
>
> Performed Fallen Test and it was negative.
>
> Yet another individual with spiritual gifts but no presence of The Fallen.
>
> He's a fine gentleman.

And with that, she closed her tablet and drove away.

189

About the Author

Robert Whitbey grew up in Shafter, CA. He attended California State University, Bakersfield, the University of Wyoming and Point Loma University. He has been a high school science teacher for over a decade and an adjunct college professor for half that time. Prior to that he spent many years working in agricultural research. His hobbies include reading, writing, gardening and golf.

He has published two prior books. His first, *How to Become a Reluctant Prepper and Why it's OK to be One*, is published under his pen name, The Reluctant Prepper. His second book and first novel, *The Angel,* is a superhero fantasy novel based in California's Central Valley.

His favorite modern authors are Peter Clines, DJ Molle and Mark Tufo.

Rob currently resides in Bakersfield, CA with his wife, Lacy, and their two sons, Dylan and Jack.

www.ingramcontent.com/pod-product-compliance
Lightning Source LLC
Chambersburg PA
CBHW071235130626
46556CB00003B/1022